Jesse Page

Samuel Crowther

the slave boy who became bishop of the Niger

Jesse Page

Samuel Crowther
the slave boy who became bishop of the Niger

ISBN/EAN: 9783744736022

Printed in Europe, USA, Canada, Australia, Japan

Cover: Foto ©Raphael Reischuk / pixelio.de

More available books at **www.hansebooks.com**

Samuel Adjai Crowther
Bishop, Niger Territory
Oct. 19 1888

THIRD EDITION. THIRTEENTH THOUSAND,

SAMUEL CROWTHER

The Slave Boy who became

BISHOP OF THE NIGER

BY

JESSE PAGE

AUTHOR OF "BISHOP PATTESON, THE MISSIONARY MARTYR OF MELANESIA."

------ ❈ ------

From out the darkness gleamed a single star,
And lo! the tempest-driven hailed its light;
So from the gloom of Afric, shone afar
The witness of the Lord, a blessed sight
Which many grateful saw, and kneeling there
Heard first the tidings of Salvation near.

------ ❈ ------

FLEMING H. REVELL COMPANY

NEW YORK   CHICAGO   TORONTO

Publishers of Evangelical Literature.

PREFACE.

THE name of Crowther is a household word in the record of missionary enterprise. The fact of his being the first native Bishop of Africa, the pathetic incidents of his early life, and the gracious success which has crowned his efforts on the banks of the Niger, have all combined to make an impress upon the memory and heart of Christian people in England which will not grow slighter with the passage of the years. Many whose eyes look upon these pages will remember the striking effect of the black Bishop's first appearance on our platforms, and will recall the more frequent occasions when in the pulpits of our churches he has pleaded the cause of the work to which he has devoted his energies and life.

But like all men of real character, to understand and appreciate Crowther you must personally know him. Few men have a more interesting and impressive individuality.

I shall never forget the rush of feeling which I experienced when in his little room at Salisbury Square I had first the privilege of seeing the subject of this biography face to face. In our many subsequent interviews this sense of heartfelt veneration increased more and more, and I recall gratefully the hours of patient and invaluable attention which he gave to the proof sheets of this work, as, word for word, I read them to him. From time to time he would arrest the reading to correct a date or even the spelling of a native name, and oftener with emotion to linger on the old scenes and explain more fully the incidents of his career as they passed in review. One of the characteristics of Bishop Crowther is a strong disapprobation of "the praise of men," and he recognised with evident pleasure that these pages aimed rather to glorify God than to magnify man.

The work on the Niger, with which his name will be for ever identified, is throughout a remarkable evidence of the advantage of employing native agency, if only to save a needless sacrifice of European lives, and at the same time exhibits what the Gospel can do, and is doing, when confronted with heathenism on the one hand and a debased form of Mohammedanism on the other. Of course the reader will not imagine that there have been no failures, no disappointments and breakdowns. In common with mission work everywhere, there have been discouragements on the Niger to try the faith and patience of the workers. But the pennon of the Cross borne aloft is still advancing, and victory is sure to those who in His name endure to the end.

At a time like the present, when the horrors of slavery are being once more forced home upon the English conscience, it is earnestly hoped that these pages may do something to awaken sympathy for the sufferings of those in direst bondage. Crowther, let it be remembered, was once a slave, and he is keenly sensitive to the woes and wretchedness of his unhappy brethren in Africa. Had it fallen within the province of this book, much, very much more, might have been said about slavery,—it has been indeed difficult to repress a reference to the horrible tidings of deeds done in Africa which week after week shock even the most prosaic of us by their vileness. The knocks at the door of the English heart, once so lightly moved, are many to-day. Cardinal Lavigérie, Lieutenant Wissman, and others, speak of that which they have seen until our hearts are faint with the sickening re-cital, and last not least, Commander Cameron in a recent article says, " The time has now come when we can no longer plead ignorance ; from missionaries of every branch of the Catholic Church of Christ we hear of the sufferings of the negro. Those who would raise the native races, and abolish slavery by the introduction of the arts of peace and the extension of legitimate commerce, have been attacked by the slave dealers, and a gentleman holding the position of British Consul has been stripped of his clothes, and flouted and jeered at by the traders in human flesh." Then he closes with a declaration which does honour to his spirit, " I am ready to act up to what I write, and would freely give my life in the cause of freedom, and will gladly co-operate in any possible manner, either here or in Africa, with those who, I trust, will resolve that this disgrace to humanity shall no longer exist."

The observations of Bishop Crowther on that other curse of Africa, Mohammedanism, in these pages, will well repay the reader's consideration. Few men have had a closer experience of the real teaching and practice of Islam than he, and even his charitable mind cannot credit it with the philosophic sweetness and light with which it is the fashion in some quarters to invest the religion of the false prophet. It must not be forgotten that this religion is that of the slave driver and slave killer throughout the Dark Continent.

It only remains for me to acknowledge with thanks the great courtesy I have received from the Church Missionary Society, in having placed at my disposal the journals and other literary material out of which this work has been constructed. Without this invaluable assistance at Salisbury Square these pages could not have been written,

JESSE PAGE.

Introductory note by Bishop Crowther

By desire of the author of this work
I have perused the proof sheets with him and can
testify to their being a true and faithful record of
my life and work, as circumstances caused their brief
statements in report.

Looking back upon my many and eventful
years, I see abundant reason for thankfulness to the
Giver of every good and perfect gift, and to say from
my heart, "Hitherto hath the Lord helped me." He has
graciously kept me from the hour when as a little
slave-boy, I was providentially saved from a life
of misery and ignorance of Himself, and brought
into contact with the Christian faith, through the
instrumentality of the British Government, and
the Christian and persevering labour of the Church
Missionary Society in faithful obedience to the command
of our ascended Lord, "Go and teach all nations."

If through my imperfect labour the work
of God has been advanced on the Niger, the praise
be all ascribed to Him and not to me. I cannot
expect to labour many years more in the cause of
Christ which lies so near my heart, but it is my
earnest prayer that these pages may be the means
of leading others to enter the harvest field of Africa,
or at any rate to support prayerfully and gene-
rously, the workers already labouring for the great
Head of the Church in my native land.

Samuel Adjai Crowther.

Oct 1888

God speed thee!
Though weary weight of years be thine,
Strong is thine heart, while rays Divine
Upon thy pathway ever shine.

God speed thee!
To the sad sinner's heart of pain,
To the poor slave in Satan's chain;
Tell Christ hath died and risen again.

God speed thee!
He knows their suffering and their fears,
He hears their sighing, counts their tears,
For Afric's children Jesus cares.

God speed thee!
Strengthen thine hand to battle on,
Brave to contend, till from the Throne,
Falls on thine ear the glad "Well done."

God speed thee!
Thy day of work will soon be o'er,
Then comes the eve of rest, and sure
The dawn of life for evermore.

CONTENTS.

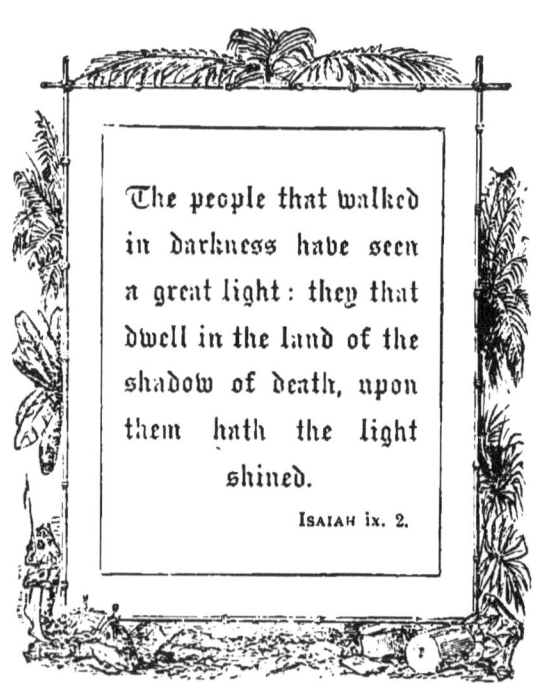

The people that walked in darkness have seen a great light: they that dwell in the land of the shadow of death, upon them hath the light shined.

ISAIAH ix. 2.

SAMUEL CROWTHER.

CHAPTER I.

THE HOME-LAND OF THE SLAVE.

" From Greenland's icy mountains,
  From India's coral strand,
Where Afric's sunny fountains
  Roll down their golden sand ;
From many an ancient river,
  From many a palmy plain
They call us to deliver
  Their land from error's chain."—HEBER.

For centuries the history of Africa has been the mystery and sorrow of the world. Up to a time still fresh in the memory of our grandfathers the map of the Dark Continent, dark in more senses than one, gave little trouble to the schoolboy, being simply an irregular coast-line enclosing wide spaces in blank, trespassed upon by lines of almost guess-work boundaries, and in the middle thereof sundry high places denoted by the romantic title of the Mountains of the Moon.

Its history is, strange to say, of the oldest and the youngest. Amid the sands of its northern deserts we turn up the relics of a civilization which astonished Joseph and his brethren, while our knowledge of the interior is but the discovery of yesterday. A weird mystery hangs over this marvellous land; we know not whether our next step will reveal the dim shadowy life of a day when the world was in its early spring, and awaken the echoes of a past unknown.

If it were the purpose of the present work to revive the memories of Africa's remote glories, especially when its Christian martyrs and teachers swelled the roll of the early Church, much might be told of enthralling interest; but we have in these pages to tell the story of our own time. And yet the better to understand our ground, we must glance back at the growth of our acquaintance with the Dark Continent during the last two or three centuries.

It seems remarkable that for so many years the traders who were the only European visitors to its shores should have remained contented with a knowledge of the very fringe of that vast land, making few if any efforts to penetrate into the interior. For the discovery of the coast-line credit must be given to the Portuguese, whose stately galleons in the fifteenth century touched in turn at the Canary Islands, Cape Verd, Sierra Leone, the Cape of Good Hope, and round eastward up as far as Cape Guardafui.

It was two hundred years later that the Dutch settled in the southern districts, where still their nationality makes itself known and felt. Nothing seems to have been added to our store of information about Africa until comparatively recent times, when

our own countrymen began to search for the source of
the Nile. Neither the philosopher's stone nor the North
Pole can boast of more ardent and spirited discoverers
than those brave explorers, who under privations and
perils sought the secret spot where the bubbling waters
of the Nile first rushed forth amid tangled grasses and
fronded palms on their way to the sea. Bruce traced
the Blue Nile along its devious course at the end of the
last century; but it was only a little more than
twenty-five years ago that Speke on his second journey
sent home the message, "The Nile is settled," as
Grant and he stood on the shores of that magnificent inland lake, the Victoria Nyanza, from which
mighty source the ancient river of Egypt evidently
flows.

Before then, however, other rivers had been traced
at the price of precious lives, notably the Niger,
which Mungo Park sighted in 1796, and afterwards
Denham, Clapperton, Laing and Lander; the Congo
where Tuckey died in 1830, and the Zambesi, by
whose banks David Livingstone, in 1854, made his
brave and patient way while traversing the Continent.
But in these later days the "eye to business" motive
has quickened interest and exploration, and European
States are scrambling for allotments of the black
man's land.

Of the people, we know enough to awaken our pity
rather than our admiration. If they are accounted
naturally indolent, it is because in their native
condition there is no necessity to put forth energy,
save in war. A distinguished man, who has recently
visited them, assures us that when an opportunity
presents itself they can work as hard and more

patiently than others. Their intellectual capacity,
and painstaking studies, the subsequent pages of
this book will verify in the life of one of Africa's
worthiest sons.

Many have treated the black man as having no
mind, and more have virtually denied him a soul.
That he has both, however, is the growing conviction
of the Christian Church to-day, and she is anxious
to vindicate her responsibility in support of this. The
spiritual condition of the Africans is curious and
distressing. Taking the population to be about two
hundred millions, quite three-fourths of them are
utter heathen, living in the densest darkness of
superstition and sin. The immense majority of the
other fourth are followers of the false prophet, and
the spiritual conquest of Africa by the green flag of
Mohammed is still actively pressed to-day.

There are a few Jews living on the shores of the
blue Mediterranean Sea, and of course Christianity
is not without its witnesses. Also, besides the
Roman Catholics and Protestants, there are the
Copts and Abyssinians. But, speaking generally,
the natives of Africa profess two religions, one of
Mohammed, the False Prophet, and the other of the
Devil in multiplication. Of the former we shall have
something to say in the later pages of this work, for
it is the key to much of the misery of this sad land.
But even in those districts where Mohammedanism has
got the firmest hold, it has not superseded, but rather
grafted itself upon the superstitious demon worship
of the natives everywhere.

In a fearfully real sense, to the African "the things
which are seen are temporal, and the things which

are not seen are eternal." His terror is the environ-
ment of evil spirits, peopling the air, hiding in the
trees, whispering in the wavelets of the stream, seated
on the crest of every hill, and lurking in the rank
grasses of the plain. From this ubiquitous company
of devils the poor negro can never hope to be free.

We have only then to add, that these satanic
agencies are all credited with a vindictive hatred to
the human race, to complete the picture of unspeak-
able and oppressive horror which crouches like a
nightmare upon the hearts of the African people. In
their wretched dread they are for ever making friends
with these demons, propitiating them not unfre-
quently with the sacrifice of human life.

No wonder, then, that witchcraft is everywhere, and
that the medicine man, like the Romish prelate of the
Middle Ages, can strike a terrified submission even
into the heart of kings. Tetzel with his indulgence
business never did so well as they ; to make a charm
nothing comes amiss—a stone, a bit of bone or filthy
rag, a shell, a leaf, an animal or a piece of it, any of
these will do as a fetish, with power to exorcise the
evil spirit. The priest's hand, true of superstition
everywhere, has in Africa its black grasp on the
substance of the poor.

Here, too, is evidence of that declaration of Holy
Writ, that "the dark places of the earth are full of
the habitations of cruelty." The "customs" of the
country show an utter disregard of human life; and
in the western districts, with which these pages will
have more especially to do, it will be seen that a
wholesale slaughter often follows the death of a
king, in order that he may be suitably accompanied

to the land of shadows. The cruel and pitiless character of paganism is here fully revealed.

In one respect, at least, the superstitious fear of the poor African is well founded, for upon his country has settled an evil spirit in verity and truth, and that demon is called *Slavery*. In the mere mention of that word, with the knowledge of what it means, one realises how weak at the strongest is language to express the truth. Words of burning flame are wanted to describe this awful curse. There was a time when the hearts of the English people were thrilled and shocked with their own responsibility in the matter, and we made perhaps the costliest sacrifice in history for the sake of moral principle. It became high time to act. A hundred years ago our ships carried their share of 38,000, out of 74,000 slaves, exported annually, and Granville Sharp sent the Lord Chancellor a cutting from a newspaper, advertising the sale of a black girl, at a public-house in the Strand! There is no need to tell the story over again. Wilberforce as well as Wellington will be never forgotten, for "peace hath her victories as well as war." The patient and prayerful agitation of years was crowned by the passing of an Act of Parliament, which struck the fetters from the slave on English ground. Immediately our cruisers appeared in African waters to capture the slave dhows, and set the living freights at liberty.

But while curtailed by our watchfulness of the coast, the trade in "black ivory" still throve, and we are ashamed to say thrives still, in the interior of Africa. To arrest this we have spent lives more precious than gold. One of the first, best, and noblest friends Africa

ARABS BUYING SLAVES IN THE MARKET.

ever had, David Livingstone, telling his countrymen of the desolating wrongs of the slave trade, besought them to "heal this open sore of the world." And when weary with his wanderings he laid himself down to die on the grass at Ilala, he breathed his last, as he would have wished, on the soil of the land for which he had worked and prayed. And Gordon too, the fearless Christian knight whose very name makes the heart beat more quickly, all the world knows how in Lower Egypt he drove back what seemed the irresistible progress of Arab slave-trading; and in his supreme moment of victory and defeat he also poured out his blood upon the desert sand of that Africa he loved so well.

We have called it the home-land of the slave because from its shores he is dragged a helpless and illtreated exile. With all its pains and sorrows it is still his home. To it in many a moment of lonely and distant captivity he turns his thoughts again, and on the threshold of another world his longings lie towards Africa. Longfellow has beautifully expressed this in his well-known poem, a few verses of which shall close this chapter.

> Beside the ungathered rice he lay,
>   His sickle in his hand ;
> His breast was bare, his matted hair
>   Was buried in the sand,
> Again in the mist and shadow of sleep
>   He saw his native land.
>
> Wide through the landscape of his dreams
>   The lordly Niger flowed,
> Beneath the palm trees in the plain
>   Once more a king he strode,
> And heard the tinkling caravans
>   Descend the mountain road.

He saw once more his dark-eyed queen
  Among her children stand,
They clasped his neck, they kissed his cheek,
  They held him by the hand !
A tear burst from the sleeper's lids,
  And fell into the sand.

     *   *   *   *   *

'The forest with their myriad tongues
  Shouted of liberty ;
And the blast of the desert cried aloud,
  With a voice so wild and free,
That he started in his sleep and smiled
  At their tempestuous glee.

He did not feel the driver's whip
  Nor the burning heat of day,
For death had illumined the land of sleep,
  And his lifeless body lay
A worn out fetter which the soul
  Had broken and thrown away.

CHAPTER II.

A CHILDHOOD OF SLAVERY.

———✳———

"Let the Indian, let the Negro,
Let the rude barbarian see,
That Divine and glorious conquest
Once obtained on Calvary.
Let the Gospel
Loud resound from pole to pole."—WILLIAMS.

———✳———

HAVING now glanced at Africa as a whole, we will
set our foot upon the banks of the lordly Niger,
which will be the scene of the wonderful story of
God's providence and grace which this volume seeks
to tell. This river, second only in depth and importance to the Nile, cannot boast of a like classic history;
but it is now full of memories of faithful work and
endeavour, none the less valuable or interesting that
they pertain to the present century.

All round the Dark Continent, with few breaks, is
an invisible rampart of pestilence, the fever boundary
which no European can attempt to pass without a
risk, and often a loss, of life. In some places, however,
the danger is deepest; and because this is true of the

Gold Coast, it has been aptly and pathetically called "the white man's grave." At this point the Niger enters the sea, not with a broad expanse of rushing water like most rivers, but spreading out into a number of outlets as it slowly creeps through thickets of mangrove trees, over stretches of poisonous slime to the ocean. This forms the Niger delta, spreading along the shore for over one hundred and twenty miles.

A French traveller, M. Adolphe Burdo, has vividly described this terrible labyrinth of creeks, in which utterly lost and disheartened his Kroomen despaired. Again and again did they attempt some new passage, pushing their way between the interlacing mangrove branches along which the serpents crawled. A more desolate region can hardly be imagined.

In its course of nearly two thousand miles this river waters some of the most degraded and unhappy districts of Africa. Between its western arm and the sea-coast lies the country of the Yoruba people, natives who have suffered more perhaps than other tribes from the desolations and cruelties of the slave trade. The people pride themselves on a remote ancestry, and Captain Clapperton was informed, by a curious geographical work he met with, written by a chief, that the Yoruba nation "originated from the remnant of the children of Canaan, who were of the tribe of Nimrod." Whether this be founded on fact or not, it is enough for us to know that out of this dark region God caused a light to shine, and called forth one who should become a shepherd to these souls. A stream of life history starting from the humblest source, and with these lowly beginnings, the career of Bishop Crowther commenced to unfold.

Early in the year 1821, in the midst of the Eyó or Yoruba country, a devastating war was being waged. The army of the Mohammedan Foulah tribe, swelled by a miscellaneous crowd of escaped slaves and man-stealers, ravaged the country to right and left. Sweeping everything before them, they came at last to Oshogun, a flourishing town mustering three thousand fighting men. The ill-fated inhabitants had no warning. In most of the huts the women were peacefully preparing the morning meal, and the men were either absent or had no time to seize their weapons. Fierce warriors surrounded the fence which protected the town. A short, sharp struggle ensued; the six gates were broken through, and the victors poured into the town. Here all was panic and despair. Terrified women caught up their little ones, and bidding the elder children to follow, tried to escape in the bush. In many cases, however, they fatally impeded themselves with baggage from their huts. The Foulahs swiftly pursued them, flinging lassoes over their heads and drawing them half-choked back into their hands.

In one of the huts at this supreme moment rushed again a father to beg his family to flee; and then, the warning given, he hurried back to the front to die in their defence. His wife, like the others, hastened to the bush with her little niece and three children; one an infant of ten months, and the eldest a boy of twelve years and a half, who, child as he was, valiantly seized his bow and arrows to protect them. This little fellow was Adjai, the future Bishop of the Niger. They too, however, in their turn, were captured, and, tied together with ropes, were led out of the burning town.   As they passed along the blazing streets they saw many wounded and dying men lying, where they had been struck down, at their own doors.

After twenty miles' weary marching they reached a town, and caught a glimpse of some of their relations in

FOULAH CAPTURING LITTLE ADJAI.

the same miserable plight. The usual barbarities of the slave-march followed. The old and infirm, being no longer able to respond to the whips of their captors, were mercilessly killed, or left, with less compassion, on the wayside to die of hunger and exposure. At midnight

they reached the town of Iseh-n, where to their great
relief, as the morning broke, they were freed from their
galling ropes and hurried in a body into the presence of
the chief. He forthwith began to allot them as slaves
and spoil of war to his warriors. That is, one half
were claimed by the chief, and the other half by the
soldiers. Little Adjai and his sister became the
property of the chief; his mother, with her infant in
arms, was quickly transferred to other hands. This
was the first time the little lad had been separated
from his mother, and great of course was his grief.

The boy was exchanged for a horse, but the bargain
not being satisfactory, he was taken to the slave
market of Dah'-dah, where to his great delight he met
with his mother again, and for three months enjoyed
comparative liberty, having the precious privilege of
seeing his parent whenever he wished. But one sad
evening a man came and suddenly bound him, and
he was carried away on the march again. By his
side trudged another little boy, who had also been
torn from the arms of his mother, and cried bitterly.
They were dragged along for several days, one hand
being chained to their neck; then Adjai was sold to a
Mohammedan woman, and with her travelled to the
Popo country, on the coast where the Portuguese came
to buy slaves. As he passed on his way, towns and
villages smoked in the ruin which the enemy had
wrought, and in some of the market-places five or six
heads were nailed to the large trees as a warning to
all who did not willingly submit.

Although his mistress was kind to her little captive
boy, a great dread seized upon his mind; and he
determined to destroy himself, sooner than be sold

THE SLAVE MARCH.

into the hands of the white man. It seems very shocking that the thought of suicide should gloom the mind of one so young; but a merciful God, who had marked him out as a chosen vessel in His service, overruled and prevented the rash intention. Though he tried to strangle himself with his waistband, his courage failed him when he held the noose in his hand; and it is remarkable that the thought of using a knife, which was always ready at hand, never occurred to his mind.

Before very long they approached the district where the Portuguese would be prepared to treat for the purchase of slaves, and here before he saw the dreaded white men he was given a few sips of the white man's evil spirit, a strong and unpurified rum. Then, still pinioned to prevent escape, the little slave boy was brought to the edge of a river; and as this was the first time he had seen so much water, he was much terrified thereat. So paralysed with fear was he that he could not obey the command of his driver to enter the stream to reach the boat, so he was lifted in bodily, and hid himself among some corn bags in the bottom of the canoe. The night came on, and through these fearful hours poor little Adjai expected every minute would be his last. Dreadful indeed was his terror at the sound of the waves as they dashed against the sides of the canoe. He had no more desire to end his career, as he had purposed, by casting himself overboard.

Having reached the other side of the river, he was, with his fellow-slaves, allowed his liberty, for escape was impossible. After landing he was then employed as storekeeper at his master's house at Lagos.

Then, for the first time, he encountered the white man, a spectacle as curious and alarming to him as the first impressions of a black man would be to a European boy. This Portuguese, who eventually purchased him, made a close examination of the points of little Adjai, as he would of a horse, and then, with a number of other unhappy captives, he was attached by a padlock round his neck to a long chain, very heavy and distressing to bear. Here they were stowed in a barracoon, or slave hut, almost suffocated with the heat, and on the slightest provocation cruelly beaten with long whips.

Early one morning they were hurriedly placed on board a slaver, one hundred and eighty seven in number, packed in fearful contact in the hold, the living and the dying and the dead. Sea-sickness, hunger, thirst, and the blows of their inhuman masters made these poor half-expiring wretches long for the end. But just at this extremity of suffering and helplessness came God's provided opportunity.

Two English men-of-war, cruising about the coast, caught sight of the slave-ship and gave chase. A brief resistance, and the sailors boarded her decks and at once liberated her human cargo, transhipping them to the men-of-war. The master and slave-drivers were placed in irons, and the black men, hardly yet realising that they were in the hands of friends, stood on the British decks looking on with astonishment, not unmingled with fear.

An amusing instance of their suspicious and groundless misgivings was that they mistook the sight of a hog, partly cut up and hanging to the rigging, for the body of one of their own fellows, which the

English were going to eat. This idea was further strengthened by the appearance of a number of cannon balls, which they concluded must be the heads of their unfortunate comrades. Soon, however, they were relieved on this score, and showed in every way they could the gratitude which was in their hearts for their liberation from such cruel bondage.

The two vessels, full of freed slaves, made for Sierra Leone. One was wrecked in a storm, and lost all hands, including one hundred and two slaves; the other, with Adjai on board, reached Bathurst in safety.

Here is a wonderful indication of the working of the Divine overruling of events. One of the vessels which had captured the slaver was H.M.S. Myrmidon, and upon the deck, engaged in rescuing little Adjai and his companions was a young officer, whose son years afterwards was the devoted and useful Lieutenant Shergold Smith, the leader of the missionary enterprise on Lake Nyanza.

Shortly afterwards Adjai and the other slaves were sent from Freetown, whither they had been taken, to Bathurst, and returned for a short time in order to give evidence against their former Portuguese owners; then, coming back, they were placed under wise and kindly care. But it will be necessary, in order to clearly understand why this provision was already made for the reception of these poor slaves, to retrace a few steps of history.

The long struggle of twenty years to impress the mind of England with the horrors and inhumanity of the traffic in flesh and blood was becoming more and more desperate. The famous decision of Lord Chief

Justice Mansfield had been delivered in 1772. Thirteen years later Thomas Clarkson drew public attention to the subject by his prize essay at Cambridge University. Long before the passing of the Act, the agitation in the interest of the slave was carried on by the Abolition Society; and in 1787 Mr. Granville Sharp took charge of a crowd of four hundred negroes, and formed a settlement for them on the West Coast of Africa. This projecting piece of land, from its resemblance to a lion, received the name of Sierra Leone; and here, where slavery had hitherto been most prevalent, a colony had been formed under British protection as a rescue home for liberated Africans. But the congregation of so many degraded and lawless men soon  produced anarchy and trouble in the colony, the moral condition of the blacks was disgraceful, and the prospects of the success of the enterprise seemed very remote. However, what man cannot do God will accomplish, and in 1816 missionaries were sent thither by the Church Missionary Society; and after

much toil and constantly recurring deaths of the devoted workers, the blessing of the Almighty was seen.
In 1822 the Lord Chief Justice publicly stated that
in a population of 10,000 there were only six cases for
trial, and not one from any village under the super-
intendence of a village schoolmaster. This gratifying
fact was noted at the very time when the future
Bishop of the Niger, then a little liberated slave-boy,
had been landed at the place.

The climate was found to be most deadly for
Europeans, and during the first twenty years of the
Mission fifty-three missionaries or their wives had
succumbed to the malaria. But as fast as gaps
were made in the army of brave hearts, others came
from England to fill their place; and so by constantly renewing the earnest helpers, the work was
graciously crowned with success.

Little Adjai exhibited a proficiency for study, and
under the care of the Mission schoolmaster made
good progress. We are told that when his first day
at school was over he hastened into the town and
begged a halfpenny from one of the negroes to buy
an alphabet card, all for himself. He became in time
a monitor, and received for that official position
sevenpence-halfpenny a month; but, best of all, it
was here that the word of the Lord came unto the
little freed slave, and gave him a liberty from the
condemnation of sin which filled his heart with new
joy. He was baptized on the 11th December, 1825,
by the Rev. J. Raben, taking the name of Samuel
Crowther, by which name we shall henceforth speak
of him as we pass along his interesting and useful
career.

CHAPTER III.

ON THE THRESHOLD OF THE WORK.

———✳———

" O for a thousand tongues to sing
 My great Redeemer's praise,
The glories of my God and King,
 The triumphs of His grace.

" My gracious Master and my God,
 Assist me to proclaim,
To spread through all the earth abroad,
 The honours of Thy name."—WESLEY.

———✳———

THE wonderful improvements which followed the introduction of Christianity into the disorderly colony of freed slaves at Sierra Leone was in no small degree due to the earnest and practical efforts put forth in finding something for their idle hands and undisciplined brains to do. Trades were taught the people; and, generally speaking, notwithstanding the common imputation that the negro is naturally a lazy fellow, these liberated slaves took to their handicrafts remarkably well. We have it on the authority of Professor Drummond, who has so recently had an opportunity from his own observation of the natives of tropical Africa, that to blame the African for being lazy is a misuse of words. "He does not need to work; with so bountiful a nature round him it would be gratuitous to work. And his indolence, therefore, as it is called, is just as much a part of himself as his flat nose, and as little blameworthy as slowness is to a tortoise. The fact is Africa is a nation of the unemployed." When we free him from the forced servitude of the slave-driver we must find him employment elsewhere, and with proper tact and encouragement he will soon work away with a will.

Samuel Crowther, settling down under such patient training, was instructed in that branch of human labour which will ever be surrounded with sacred memories. As a carpenter he soon showed a proficiency in the use of the chisel and plane, and in after years this ability to work for himself and for others became exceedingly useful to him. But not only were his hands employed, but his mind began to drink with avidity from the stores of human knowledge and education. Naturally studious and intellectual, the future Bishop yearned after more light.

It is not difficult to imagine with what wild joy he received the announcement that his kind friends, Mr. and Mrs. Davey, would take him with them on a visit to England. This was in 1826; and in due time he caught the first glimpse of the white cliffs of that wonderful land about whose power and influence he had already heard so much. The ship reached Portsmouth on the 16th August; and shortly afterwards, during his stay of three or four months in London, young Adjai became a pupil in the parochial school at

Islington. These schools still remain, overlooking the leafy churchyard of the Chapel-of-Ease; but in the days when the youthful Crowther came to work for the first time by the side of English boys, Islington was still a merrie village famous for its country walks and new milk. Altogether he was not in England more than a year, but doubtless he made good use of his eyes and ears in making acquaintance with English life and manners.

Meanwhile the educational movement, inaugurated by the Church Missionary Society at Sierra Leone, was making good progress, and the Industrial Boarding School had developed into its original plan of a real Christian institution, the centre of a network of capital schools in the districts around. Hence it was proposed to utilise the place as a nursery for training native teachers, and an excellent clergyman, the Rev. C. L. F. Haensel, went out in February, 1827, to superintend its establishment. This became in due time Fourah Bay College; and the first name of the half-dozen native youths who are entered on its roll of students is that of Samuel Crowther.

As we have shown, the fatality of the climate to Europeans gave urgency to this effort to train others, who did not suffer from the same physical danger, to labour in this field. It was high time that something should be done. The Gold Coast had earned an awful name, and again and again its fever-stricken shores became whitened with the bones of the stranger. " The churchyard at Kissy," writes Bishop Vidal years afterwards, " with its multiplied memories of those not lost but gone before, is a silent but eloquent witness to the kind of schooling which the missionary

for Africa requires." Very graciously God blessed the
new venture, and it became a spiritual home from
which, from time to time, its sons sallied forth, full
of faith and zeal, to preach the unsearchable riches of
the Gospel to their brethren after the flesh.

Crowther made progress, and became an assistant
teacher in the College, and this mark of confidence and
respect was quite a turning point in his career. He
who was in the Providence of God to rise to such an
honourable position in the church, never forgot the
humility of those early days, and with gratitude he was
moved to say in a letter at this time, speaking of the
moment of his being carried into captivity:

"From this period I must date the unhappy, but
which I am ever taught in other respects to call blessed,
day which I shall never forget in my life. I call it an
unhappy day, because it was the day on which I was
violently turned out of my father's house and separated
from my relatives, and in which I was made to
experience what is called to be in slavery. With
regard to its being called blessed, it was the day
which Providence had marked out for me to set out on
my journey from the land of heathenism, superstition
and vice, to a place where the Gospel is preached."

This thankfulness, which welled up from his heart,
shaped itself into a determination, so far as God should
give him opportunity and ability, to work among his
own people, teaching them as he had been taught, and
leading them also to the Saviour who had manifested
Himself to him.

By his side, in those early and happy days at
Bathurst, a little girl, taken like himself from the deck
of a slave ship, was taught with him in the same

house. They grew up together, and in due time she being a Christian, was baptized from her native name Asano into the name of Susanna. They grew fond of each other, and after a happy period of courtship, which is the same sweet old story in Africa as elsewhere, they were married. It was the beginning

THE COLLEGE, FOURAH BAY.

of a long and blissful union, in which God blessed them with dutiful and useful children. One of them, the Rev. Dandeson Coates Crowther, is now Archdeacon of his father's diocese; two others are doing well as influential and godly laymen, and of his three daughters two have been married to native clergymen, and are their faithful helpmeets in the service of our Lord.

In the year 1830 Crowther was appointed from the College to the care of a school at Regent's Town, and his wife was officially associated with him as schoolmistress. Two years after they were promoted to still more important duties at Wellington; and finally he came back to the College on the installation of the Rev. G. A. Kissling, who afterwards became Archdeacon of New Zealand, as the new principal. Here for some years was Crowther's sphere of work; and it is gratifying to notice, that several who came under his training at this period were afterwards ordained and appointed as government chaplains at important stations on the coast.

In one respect Crowther has the same invaluable gift as Patteson, a natural aptitude for languages; and in his work at the College and elsewhere he showed how great an advantage he possessed in dealing with the chiefs and headmen of the district. This marked him out for notice at a critical moment which was approaching.

In the year 1841 the mind of England was greatly excited with a proposal, set on foot by Her Majesty's Government, to explore the river Niger. In a memorandum from Lord John Russell, then Colonial Secretary, it was explained to the Lords of the Treasury that such an expedition, suitably manned and equipped, would open up a new field for British commerce, and at the same time materially assist in putting down that infamous system of slavery which the English people so deplored. Prince Albert, then in the vigour of young manhood, and zealous as he always was of

good works, warmly espoused the idea, and the senti-
ment of the people was in its favour. It was pro
posed to give those in charge of the expedition, power,
in the Queen's name, to make contracts and enter
into agreements with the native chiefs in the direction of the abolition of the slave-trade, and the introduction of commercial relations. They were also to
establish stations, under proper protection, where
factories might be built, and where the native might
be taught a better method of trading than that of
selling slaves.

The Committee of the Church Missionary Society
quickly perceived in this undertaking an opportunity
of exploring those undiscovered territories of the
Niger, with a view to bringing the blessings of the
Gospel to those poor benighted people. The Government agreeing to this, two representatives of the
Society were appointed to accompany the expedition
—the Rev. James Frederick Schön and Mr. Samuel
Crowther. The former had, during his ten years at
Sierra Leone as a missionary, become an authority
upon the African people and their characteristics,
and of the latter little more need be said than that he
was burning to preach the Word of Life, at any sacrifice, among his own people in the far-off interior.
Happily the journals of these noble pioneers of
Christianity have been preserved, and we shall now
quote some of their own words therefrom, describing in
a most interesting manner the incidents of the voyage.

When the tidings came to Messrs. Schön and
Crowther that they were to accompany the expedition, they gladly prepared themselves for a step,
which was not unattended with prospects of danger

to themselves. The jealousy and cruelty of hostile
tribes, and the risks to health which the fearful
climate of those regions involved, faced them as
they entered upon their task. But the prospect of
preaching the Gospel to those who had never heard
of the love of Christ was a sufficient incentive to put
aside all fears. In each case, too, a separation from
wife and home was naturally painful, but most bravely
was it borne. Mrs. Schön was only just recovering
from a serious illness, and it was not until he had
prayed long and earnestly for Divine help that her
husband ventured to break the news to her of his
immediate departure.

He tells us, " This being done, I approached the bed
of my afflicted partner, and made her acquainted
with the arrival of the vessels. She was not taken
by surprise, but, on the contrary, to my astonishment, calmly replied, 'Oh! I can bear it. Never
mind me, I am only sorry that I cannot assist you
more in getting ready. Leave me, go on with your
business, God will take care of me.' To find her in such
a frame of mind was very cheering to me; I knew
well that flesh and blood could not have given it to
her, and that it was an answer to many prayers. I
learned to understand anew that it was the will of
God that I should engage in this important work.
Hitherto the Lord has removed all obstacles, and has
given me more than ordinary strength to prosecute
my preparations for it. And although I more than
ever feel my unfitness, I am not dismayed. I can lay
hold on the precious promises of God, and will go on
my way rejoicing."

Such was the spirit of one of these noble men, and

in such grand faith and self-forgetfulness did his wife bid him adieu.

With Crowther the parting was not less costly or trying to human feeling. For many reasons he experienced much reluctance to leave Fourah Bay, his College work, his home, and those dear to him. Not a few tears were secretly shed during the packing of his boxes; but on the 1st July the *Soudan* sailed, and he waved his last farewells to those on shore.

"To-day about 11 o'clock," he tells us, "the *Soudan* got under way for the Niger, the highway into the heart of Africa. She was soon followed by the *Wilberforce*, which took her in tow in order to save fuel. When I looked back on the colony in which I had spent nineteen years—the happiest part of my life, because there I was made acquainted with the saving knowledge of Jesus Christ—leaving my wife, who was near her confinement, and four children behind—I could not but feel pain and some anxiety for a time at the separation. May the Lord, who has been my guide from my youth up until now, keep them and me, and make me neither barren nor unfruitful in His service."

It was a sharp disappointment to Schön and Crowther to find that they were not to travel together, the former being attached to the *Wilberforce*, especially as they were hoping to work conjointly in their leisure in translating the Scriptures into the languages of the inland tribes. But by this arrangement we have now two distinct and most interesting accounts of the expedition, the *Wilberforce* exploring the Tshadda, and the *Soudan* passing up the main stream of the Niger.

Bearing no arms of war; equipped for no devastating conflict with the natives, but carrying a message of peace and g odwill, these English vessels steamed up the river. The brave men who stood full of hope upon their decks little dreamt how disastrous would prove their venture, and how the return of their vessels would bring but a feeble remnant back to their native land!

CHAPTER IV.

THE NIGER FIRST EXPLORED.

———✳———

" Rise, gracious God, and shine
    In all Thy saving might ;
And prosper each design
    To spread Thy glorious light.
Let healing streams of mercy flow,
    That all the earth Thy truth may know."—HURN.

———✳———

" AUGUST 20th, 1841. The *Wilberforce* and the *Soudan* (so runs Crowther's journal) got under way this morning in pursuit of the *Albert*, and in about two hours we lost sight of the sea, and were completely surrounded by thick mangroves on both sides of the creek. Apparent satisfaction was seen on every countenance, that we had now commenced our river navigation, although some could not help remarking that they were going to their graves.

" August 21. We were gradually introduced from the mangroves into a forest of palm and bamboo trees, embellished with large cotton trees of curious shapes, interspersed among them on both sides of the river, and of other lofty trees of beautiful foliage. All hands were invited on deck by this new scenery, and the day was spent with great interest at this novel appearance. We passed on both sides of the river several plantations of bananas, plantains, sugar-canes, cocoa or kalabe— so-called by the Americans—and now and then some huts with natives in them.

" The natives were so timid that they several times pulled their canoes ashore, and ran away into the bush, where they hid themselves among the grass, and peeped at the steamers with fear and great astonishment. We got opposite to a village containing about seven or eight huts, where the inhabitants in very great earnest armed themselves with sticks and country billhooks, and ran along the bank to a neighbouring village, to apprise the villagers of the dreadful approach of our wonderful floating and self-moving habitation. These villagers also followed the example of their informers. Having armed themselves in like manner, they betook themselves to the next village to bring them the same tidings. When they were encouraged to come on board, it was difficult to find persons brave enough to do so. Those who ventured to come near took care not to go further from shore than the distance of a leap from their canoe, in case there should be cause for it.

" The Captain perceiving some of them inclined to come off, stopped the engine, and persuaded them to come near us. In the meantime he had come opposite to a larger village into which all the former villagers had collected themselves. There was a little boy who acted as their interpreter because he understood two English words, ' Yes ' and ' Tabac,' which he had picked up at some place. They constantly told him

something to tell us, but he could not say anything
else besides his 'yes' and 'tabac.'

"After much hesitation a large canoe came off with
no less than forty-three persons in it. It was with
great difficulty that some of them were persuaded to
come on board. Their fear may be accounted for by
the slave-traders having often pursued their victims
through the mangrove swamp. My expectation was
greatly raised when I found among them a Yoruba boy
of about thirteen years of age, from whom I thought we
could get some information about these people; but
the poor little fellow had almost lost his native language, through his lonely situation among them. He
could not even understand me very well when I asked
him about his father and mother and his own town.
He must have travelled hundreds of miles before he
got into this secret part of Africa. Here we were
overtaken by the *Albert* and *Wilberforce*, the latter took
another branch of the river this evening to prove its
course. The *Albert* and the *Soudan* dropped anchors
about ten miles from the branch taken by the *Wilberforce*, to spend the first Sabbath of our ascent up the
Niger. Plenty of cocoanut trees were seen in many of
the villages to-day.

"August 22, the Lord's Day. We are now below a
small village quietly enjoying the Christian Sabbath.
Not more than two furlongs from us are a people who
know no heaven, fear no hell, and who are strangers
from the covenant of promise, having no hope and
without God in the world. How inexcusable art thou,
O man, who art living in a place where the gospel of
Christ is preached every Sabbath, yet who preferrest
to live in darkness, in ignorance of God, of Christ. and

of the state of thine own soul, to being made wise unto salvation by the saving knowledge of the gospel of Jesus Christ. Take care lest these people rise up in judgment against thee, and condemn thee, because thou rejectest the counsel of God against thyself.

"August 23. This morning, about half-past 5 o'clock, we got under way, leaving the *Albert* behind, as she was waiting for the return of the *Wilberforce*. We continued to pass several huts and plantations of sugar-canes, bananas, and plantains. Many natives made their appearance, and came out to us in their canoes; some being dressed in old soldiers' and drummers' coats, having on old common black hats. You scarcely can imagine how they looked in these dresses, having on neither shirt nor trousers, with the exception of a piece of cloth or handkerchief around their waists. As their coats were red and showy, they took a very great pride in their whimsical dresses. A blue flag, with fanciful figures of man, monkey, bottle, etc., was flying in one of their canoes. They were not afraid of us, for they came of their own accord, with their notes of recommendation from the captains of former steamers. After we had steamed for about two hours we came to another large village, from whence the natives soon came around us with plenty of bananas and plantains. The people here scarce want anything else in exchange for their fruits beside rum, for which they constantly call out, 'Vlolo, Vlolo!' at the same time applying their hands to their mouths, intimating to us that they wanted something to drink. But as Captain Allen would not countenance anything of the kind, we could buy very little of their things.

THE CHASE OF A SLAVE IN A MANGROVE SWAMP.

"August 29, Lord's Day. Lay at anchor yesterday, a little above Ibo, to enjoy the Sabbath, an emblem of the rest that remaineth for the people of God."

Crowther then goes on to describe his visit to king Obi, a potentate whose position and influence made the incident of his coming in contact with the expedition of much importance. A man of average size, with a pleasant smile, dressed in calico trousers and coat, and ornamented with huge strips of pipe coral, leopard's teeth and brass buttons. In order that we may better understand the king and his people we will quote from the journal of Mr. Schön, who had specially to arrange the slave treaty with him.

"King Obi sent one of his sons to welcome the strangers. He was a very fine-looking young man, about twenty years of age. Both himself and his companions attended our morning devotions, after which I told them what book it was of which I had been reading a portion, and that I had come to this country to tell the people what God had in it revealed to us. They were surprised, and could not well understand how it was possible that I should have no other object in view. They are sensible of their inferiority in every respect to white men, and can therefore be easily led by them either to do evil or good.

"When I told one this morning that the slave trade was a bad thing, and that white people wished to put an end to it altogether, he gave me an excellent answer, 'Well, if white people give up buying, black people will give up selling slaves.' He assured me, too, that it had hitherto been his belief, that it was the will of God that black people should be slaves of white people!

"This afternoon I satisfied myself of the correctness of various particulars which I had previously obtained of the Ibo people respecting some of their superstitious practices. It appears to be but too true that human sacrifices are offered by them, and that in the most barbarous manner. The legs of the devoted victim are tied together, and he is dragged from place to place till he expires. The person who gave me this information told me that one man had been dragged about for nearly a whole day before his sufferings terminated in death. The body is afterwards cast into the river. Interment is always denied them, they must become food for alligators or fishes. Sometimes people are fastened to trees or to branches close to the river until they are famished.

"Also if a child should happen to cut its top teeth first the poor infant is likewise killed; it is considered to indicate that the child, were it allowed to live, would become a very bad person. To say to any person, 'You cut your top teeth first,' is, therefore, as much as to say nothing good can be expected from you; you are born to do evil, it is impossible for you to act otherwise. . . . .

"The Ibos are in their way a religious people, the word 'Tshuku,' God, is continually heard. Tshuku is supposed to do everything. When a few bananas fell out of the hands of one into the water, he comforted himself by saying, 'God has done it.'

"Their notions of some of the attributes of the Supreme Being are in many respects correct, and their manner of expressing them striking. 'God

E

made everything. He made both white and black,' is continually on their lips. Some of their parables are descriptive of the perfections of God, when they say, for instance, that God has two eyes and two ears, that the one is in heaven and the other on earth. I suppose the conception that they have of God's omniscience and omnipresence cannot be disputed.

"On the death of a person who has in their estimation been good, they will say, ' He will see God ; ' while of a wicked person they will say, ' He will go into fire.'

"I had frequent opportunities of hearing these expressions at Sierra Leone ; and though I was assured that they had not heard them from Christians, I would not state them before I had satisfied myself by inquiring of such as had never had any intercourse with Christians, that they possessed correct ideas of a future state of reward and punishment. Truly God has not left Himself without witness !

" Another subject upon which they are generally agreed, but which I am sorry to say, I shall have no opportunity of pursuing any further, is the following : It is their common belief that there is a certain place or town in the Ibo country in which Tshuku dwells, and where he delivers his oracles and answers inquiries. Any matter of importance is left to his decision, and people travel to the place from every part of the country. It is said to be in the rainy season three months' journey from this town, but that in the dry season it could be made in a much shorter time.

" I was informed to-day that last year Tshuku had given sentence against the slave trade. The person of him is placed on a piece of ground which is immediately and miraculously surrounded by water. Tshuku cannot be seen by any human eye, his voice is heard from the ground. He knows every language on earth, makes known thieves, and if there is fraud in the heart of the inquiring he is sure to find it out, and woe to such a person, for he will never return. He hears every word that is said against him, but can only revenge himself when persons come near him. I once asked a man, ' Did the people ever drive him out of his hole?' when he said to me very seriously, ' Master, do not take such a word, perhaps by-and-by you go see the place. Tshuku will kill you. You hear now, " You must drive me out of my hole;" and the time he begin for talk you no go open your mouth again.' They sincerely believe all these things, and many others respecting Tshuku, and obey his orders implicitly ; and if it should be correct that he has said that they should give up the slave trade, I have no doubt that they will do it at once."

The native interpreter on board the *Wilberforce* was Simon Jonas, one of the liberated slaves ; and when he came amongst people who had known him they could not credit the fact of his being still alive and well. It was the prevalent notion among these natives that slaves purchased by the white people were killed and eaten, and their blood used to dye red cloth. One of these poor heathen was, at the request of the interpreter, brought on board, and Mr. Schön goes on to tell us :

"Though many years had elapsed since our interpreter was sold, and the other had in the meantime become an old man, they instantly recognised each other, and I cannot describe the astonishment manifested by the Ibo man at seeing one whom he verily believed had long since been killed and eaten by the white people. His expressions of surprise were strong, but very significant. 'If God Himself,' he said, 'had told me this I could not have believed what my eyes now see.' The interpreter then found out that Anya was the very place to which he had been first sold as a slave, and at which he had spent nine years of his early life, and that the very person with whom he was speaking had been his doctor and nurse in a severe illness, on which account he had retained a thankful remembrance of him. The Ibo man was kindly treated by the captain, and his request to be allowed to accompany us to Obi was instantly granted. He calls himself brother to Obi ; but it is well known that the word ' brother ' has a most extensive signification in Western Africa. When he was asked whether he thought that Obi would be glad to see white men, he gave a reply which I was not prepared to hear from the lips of a pagan.   'These three months,' he said, 'we have been praying to God to send white man's ship.'

"Oh that I could believe and be convinced that this was something of the cry of the Macedonians, 'Come over, and help us!' But a suspicious thought intrudes itself on my mind, and makes me suppose that it is the desire of seeing a slave dealer with his cargo in exchange for their own flesh and blood."

CHAPTER V.

A SORROWFUL RETURN.

———·❋·———

" While I draw this fleeting breath,
 When my eyes shall close in death,
 When I rise to worlds unknown,
 And behold thee on Thy throne,
 Rock of Ages cleft for me,
 Let me hide myself in Thee !"—TOPLADY.

———·❋·———

THERE are few spectacles so disappointing as that
of brave endeavour baffled by forces which it
cannot overcome, returning with its noble aim un-
accomplished. Nothing could exceed the courage and
energy displayed by those who composed this expedition up the Niger ; and although in dealing with these
native tribes, especially on such a delicate subject as
the commerce in slaves, the explorers held their lives
very cheaply, they found a foe barring their progress
which no efforts of theirs could overcome. A pesti-
lential fever, which, leaving no impression on the
natives, was rapidly fatal to Europeans, soon began
to decimate the party. It is a saddening record
of high hopes extinguished in feebleness and pain.
There seemed to be a strange fatality attaching to

the ships, and accident as well as disease was at work in impeding their progress.

Crowther tells us that when they reached the important native town of Attah, " the Ingalla interpreter, whose services were mostly needed at this place, accidently fell overboard from the *Albert*, and was drowned. I was just on the way to ask permission to go on board the *Albert*, as she was going nearer the town with all who were desirous of going on shore, when she got under way, in search of this poor man who had made himself very useful in this country. The Lord seeth not as man seeth. ' Trust not in man, whose breath is in his nostrils, for wherein is he to be accounted of.' "

It appears from what Mr. Schön says of this event, that there was reason to deplore specially the end of this man's life. He was a Christian convert, and had been a communicant for several years of the church in Sierra Leone ; and his only child, a girl of fifteen, was then a promising pupil in one of the schools. It seems, however, that on his return to his native place here he spent the night on shore against the orders of the commander, and had partaken too freely of the palm wine of the natives. Thus it is feared that on his return he was not altogether under control, and paid the awful penalty of losing his life. At his death the apathy of the natives was apparent, although the poor fellow was struggling in the water within reach of three canoes, holding at least a hundred persons, not one attempted to stretch out a hand to help him !

As the vessels approached the confluence of the Tshadda with the Niger, the country became more

hilly, and the river had overflowed its banks, flooding
the villages in the vicinity up to the tops of the huts.
But notwithstanding the pleasant scenery, the illness
which was spreading over the vessels told too plainly
how deadly was the climate. Mr. Schön tells us what
he felt at this moment.

"The country we are now in, the clear air and dry
atmosphere we now enjoy would cause us to doubt
that the climate could be dangerous, were it not for
the sick and the dying by whom we are surrounded.
I pray for them, I pray with them, and their sick-
beds have taught me many a lesson. I cannot speak
of decided cases of sick or death-bed conversions;
but I have had pleasing proofs that my feeble assistance was acceptable, and, I trust, blessed by God to
them. Of some I am certain that they have not
engaged in this expedition for the sake of double pay,
but were actuated by better and nobler motives; and
to them belongs the promise of the Saviour, that they
shall in no wise lose their reward. I feel much supported by the assurance that many prayers are offered
up in distant lands on our behalf, by the friends of
the great cause in which we have the honour to be
engaged. The heat to-day was great—87° at 5 p.m.
—but by no means oppressive. The only incon-
venience I felt arose from the want of sound sleep.
I am covered with the prickly-heat, which made me
feel all the night as if I was lying on needles.

"September 12th, Lord's Day. Another death on
board the *Albert* last night, and several persons still
very ill in each of our vessels. There is no knowing
what another day may bring forth. If ever I felt
the importance and responsibility of the minister of

the Gospel it was to-day. Our service was to my
mind a solemn one. I administered the sacrament
for the first time on board the *Wilberforce*. The service was held on the quarter-deck; behind me was
the lifeless corpse of N——, a sailor who expired last
night, before me an attentive audience of as many as
could be spared from their work. On deck were the
carpenters making a coffin; on the forecastle of the
vessel were seven persons dangerously ill of fever;
and at a few yards from us was the *Albert*, lying with
the usual sign of mourning—a lowered flag. I spoke
on the right state of mind which ought to possess us
at the approach of death. My text was taken from
Acts vii., the last two verses. It was not a studied
sermon, it came from the heart; and if I'm not mis-
taken, found its way to the heart. The sailor was
buried by myself at Adda kudda this evening. I
heard of no new case of sickness to-day, and was
thankful when I observed that some of our people
were to all appearance improving. I could truly and
fully enter into the feelings of one man when he told
me that he hoped by God's mercy to be spared and
permitted to see his wife and child once more. The
chord of sympathy was powerfully touched by his
expression of this desire."

One of the most serious aspects of this fever was
that the medical men attached to the expedition were
beginning to suffer themselves; and one of them, Mr.
Nightingale, the surgeon on the *Albert*, was mortally
struck down. He was a young and particularly healthy
man, with a prospect of being very useful, and learned
in his profession. One of the two missionaries was
with him in his dying moments, and was led to believe

from his last words that the Saviour of sinners was precious to him. Fifty-five persons were now lying helpless on the decks of the ship, and from time to time they were added to the number of the dead. Where they had hoped to bring the blessing of Christian teaching they found only a grave, and a piece of land was purchased from the king of Attah as a burial ground, where Dr. Nightingale and others were interred. A deep solemnity rested on the crews, and the morning and evening prayers became times of impressive feeling. As the shadows drew on and night closed in they sang with heart-breaking emotion and yet a reviving faith,

> " Why do we mourn departing friends,
>   Or shake at death's alarms ?
> 'Tis but the voice that Jesus sends
>   To call them to His arms."

At last the captains being laid low, urgent steps were necessary, and it was decided that the *Soudan*, with a mournful cargo of invalids, should turn and glide with all haste back to the sea. With it Crowther returned; and he tells us how dispiriting was that journey, in which the two brave leaders, Captain Trotter and Captain Allen, were lying side by side in dangerous sickness. Death passed among the suffering, and again and again they had to consign their bodies to the deep; while many of those who lived on raged in delirium, and in one or two cases flung themselves from the ships in the madness of fever. The *Wilberforce* followed on the homeward track shortly afterwards, a moving hospital, with scarcely enough strength on board to direct its passage down the river.

The *Albert*, however, with a very small staff, was

CONFLUENCE OF THE NIGER AND TSHADDA, WEST AFRICA.

ordered to pursue her way up stream, and upon her decks was Mr. Schön. With varying experiences they pursued their way, coming in contact with the Nufi people; observing everywhere the terror exhibited at the oppression by the Fulatahs, and having a most interesting and encouraging interview with Rogan, an old chief, at Egga. The Mohammedans had it all their own way in these districts, and the Mallams who represented that religion treated Mr. Schön very courteously, giving him copies of their Arabic books, which, however, they were not able themselves to read. Much valuable information was obtained as to the sale of slaves; of service to those who came afterwards. But death pointed once more with bony finger down the stream, and commanded them to return. We read in Mr. Schön's journals:

"October 4th. 'Hitherto shalt thou come and no further,' was the message of this morning. 'Draw up the anchor and return to the sea as fast as possible.' I always apprehended this. My feelings naturally opposed it continually, and the thought of it grieved my heart; but now I feel reconciled to it, seeing that it is the only resource left to us. Captain Trotter was taken ill last evening, and the symptoms of fever were too plain this morning to favour the hope that it was merely a momentary indisposition. Only one European officer was able to perform duty on board. The fever on the others has not subdued; and not one will be able to do duty for some time, even should their lives be spared, which at present appears very doubtful.

"We made but little progress to-day in our return to the sea, as there was some business going on at

Egga, and the engineers being still ill, steam could not be got up. Captain Trotter, I am thankful to say, appeared better this afternoon; but the other invalids, I am sorry to add; were apparently no better. May their valuable lives be preserved for the good of the cause in which they are zealously labouring.

"October 5th. All of us were disturbed last night by the illness of several of our companions, but especially by one, who, in a state of delirium, continued making a great noise up to one o'clock this morning. In the gun-room we surrounded the dying bed of Lieutenant Stenhouse, expecting every moment to see him yield up his spirit unto God who gave it. He was partially delirious, but there was a great contrast in his conduct to that of the others: the former cried, 'We are all lost—we are all lost—God Almighty has said it;' while the lieutenant was as meek and gentle as a lamb, and his expressions betrayed grief on account of sin, and at times indicated some enjoyment of the consolations of the Gospel.

"He said, 'God be merciful to me, Christ died for me. Thy kingdom come!' Seizing my hand, he said, 'God bless you! God be with you. I thank you.'

"Captain B. Allen seemed better in health this morning. He is always in an excellent frame of mind; all the Christian graces shine in him. He says, and, with the Apostle, feels what he says to be true, 'For me to live is Christ, and to die is gain;' and if there be a prevailing desire in his mind it certainly is, 'rather to be absent from the body and to be present with the Lord.' O enviable state of mind! May my soul be seeking more and more to be in such a state!"

The intense trouble which wrung the heart of Mr.

Schön may be seen in the following extract written at the moment of their sad return, when he says that the whole result of the expedition may be written in one terrible word, "*failure !* "

" I long for better days, and for a change in our condition. I have endured personal sufferings, family afflictions, sore and grievous, and witnessed and shared in the trials of others during my residence of eight years in Sierra Leone, but nothing that I have hitherto seen or felt can be compared with our present condition. Pain of body, distress of mind, weakness, sorrow, sobbing, and crying, surround us on all sides. The healthy, if so they may be called, are more like walking shadows than men of enterprise. Truly, Africa is an unhealthy country ! When will her redemption draw nigh ? All human skill is baffled— all human means fall short. Forgive us, O God, if in these we have depended and been forgetful of Thee, and let the light of Thy countenance again shine upon us that we may be healed ! "

In due time they sighted the other ship, and a new life thrilled the blood of the poor invalids as it was announced to them that the sea glittered in the distance. The salt breath of the ocean seemed to bring energy back again ; but alas, to many it was but the flicker of life's expiring flame! With hearts full of deep thankfulness, Mr. Schön and Mr. Crowther met each other once more ; and thus ended the fatal and sorrowful enterprise known as the first Niger expedition. So great was the disappointment and regret in England that for twelve years public opinion would not allow another expedition to follow it.

CHAPTER VI.

An Unexpected and Happy Meeting.

————✳————

" Tell it out among the heathen that the Saviour reigns !
  Tell it out !   Tell it out !
Tell it out among the nations, bid them burst their chains !
  Tell it out !   Tell it out !
Tell it out among the weeping ones that Jesus lives,
Tell it out among the weary ones what rest He gives ;
Tell it out among the sinners that He came to save,
Tell it out among the dying that He triumphed o'er the grave.'
                                          Havergal.

————✳————

Although the first Niger expedition had closed so dis-
astrously, there was one fact which it evidenced
most satisfactorily, namely, that Samuel Crowther had
within him the stuff of which a true missionary is
made, and was entitled to be ranked among those
glorious witnesses for Christ who are charged with the
message of mercy to heathen lands.   In many hours
of trial and suffering, when the crews of the ill-fated
vessels lay around the decks in agony, Crowther
showed the sympathy of a Christian minister, and his
words were not unfruitful at such a trying time.
There was also shown in his treatment of the chiefs
of the various tribes the advantage of negotiating

through one of their own colour and country, and whatever success did attend the efforts put forth in establishing good relations with the natives was largely due to the services of the future Bishop of the Niger. Combining courage with gentleness, and possessing no small show of that patient tact which is indispensable in dealing with these people, Crowther won his spiritual spurs under these trying circumstances. It was also very satisfactory to find that while the white people were prostrate with sickness, Crowther maintained his thoughts and vigour, demonstrating beyond question the importance of working such a dangerous field with native agency.

It is not surprising, therefore, that on his return to Fourah Bay College, Mr. Schön wrote to the Committee of the Church Missionary Society in London, pointing out Crowther's usefulness and ability, and recommending them to prepare him for ordination. In accordance with this he was recalled to England, and on the 3rd of September 1842, landed again upon our shores.

During this voyage he had busied himself with his translations, and had prepared a grammar and vocabulary of the Yoruba tongue, which was afterwards of the greatest service in spreading the Gospel among those of his own people and country. He came to the Highbury Missionary College, in the Upper Street, Islington, which was then under the able care of Rev. C. F. Childe. Here he prosecuted his studies, and in due time, on Trinity Sunday, June 11th, 1843, he received at the hands of the Bishop of London (Dr. Blomfield) the rite of ordination, the first of several native clergy who were then dedicating themselves to the service of the Lord.   After four months of diaconate he was admitted into full orders as a minister of Christ's flock.

It was the beginning of a new era in missionary enterprise, and the good Bishop in his sermon on behalf of the Society, referred to it in these terms of appreciation and gratitude :—

"What cause for thanksgiving to Him, who hath made of one blood all nations of men, is to be found in the thought that has not only blessed the labourers of the Society by bringing many of those neglected and persecuted people to the knowledge of a Saviour, but that from among a race who were despised as incapable of intellectual exertion and acquirement, He has raised up men well qualified, even in point of knowledge, to communicate to others the saving truths which they have themselves embraced, and to become preachers of the Gospel to their brethren according to the flesh."

As soon as possible Crowther was on his way to Africa; and it was on the 2nd December, 1843, that once more he stepped on shore at Sierra Leone, and on the Sunday following preached his first sermon in English to the crowded assembly of native Christians which filled the church.   His text was appropriately, "And yet there is room," and he spoke, as it were, the pioneer word of faith and hope in his new work.   At the close of the sermon he administered the sacrament to a large number of negroes, and when he got home penned the following words in his journal :

"December 3rd.   Preached my first sermon in Africa. . ♦ . The novelty of seeing a native clergyman performing divine service excited a very great interest

F

among all who were present. But the question, 'Who maketh thee to differ?' filled me with shame and confusion of face. It pleases the Disposer of all hearts to give me favour in the sight of His people, and wherever I go they welcome me as a messenger of Christ."

Not long afterwards he preached again, but in his native Yoruba; and among a crowd of rescued slaves he proclaimed in their own language the wonderful works and mercy of God. At the close they all heartily responded with "Ke oh sheh," their equivalent for our "Amen."

We have already seen, in giving the details of Crowther's capture as a slave, how fiercely the Foulah race were devastating the Yoruba people. The object of these wars seems to have been simply to supply men for the slave-market, and to effect this, three hundred native towns were ruthlessly destroyed. But such oppression could not for ever be pursued; so we find that the several refugees gathered together finally at a spot where a huge rock, called Olumo, lifted up its head as with a protective air, and there they founded a great city, four miles in diameter, and with a population of 100,000 souls, called Abeokuta, or "under the stone." They strongly fortified their position; and being only seventy miles from their port of Badagry, a trade soon began to be established between their city and Sierra Leone. Some of those who returned from the latter place to Abeokuta were baptized Christians, and they begged that a missionary might be sent to them. Mr. Henry Townsend was therefore despatched thither, and received from the principal chief, Shodeké, a very cordial reception. Thus in 1844 the Yoruba Mission was begun, and Crowther, with Mr. Göllmer, another missionary, went there to establish this work, taking with them their wives and children, with interpreters and native catechists.

They were detained for eighteen months at Badagry; and while there learned with some dismay that the friendly chief Shodeké was dead, although they soon received from his successor a hearty welcome. During this enforced stay at Badagry they worked hard among the people. Crowther translated the Scriptures into Yoruba, and preached the Gospel to a large war camp which was established in the district. The door of opportunity which eventually opened for them to go up like men to take the city in Christ's name was singularly unclosed by a slave dealer. This man was finding his infamous trade suffering, so he sent £200 in presents to the chief at Abeokuta, offering more in return for slaves. With this Crowther sent a messenger to the new chief, Sagbua, and immediately the road was opened and the missionaries entered Abeokuta on August 3rd, 1846. Great rejoicings followed their arrival, the Christians especially hailing with delight teachers who would instruct them and build up their Church. And here, after three weeks, there occurred an incident in the life of Crowther, which is perhaps one of the most pathetic and interesting this book can record. It was the meeting with his mother. We cannot refrain from telling the story in his own words.

"August 21. The text for this day in the Christian Almanac, is 'Thou art the Helper of the fatherless.' I have never felt the force of this text more than I did this day, as I have to relate that my mother, from whom I was torn away about five-and-twenty years ago, came with my brother in quest of me. When she saw me she trembled. She could not believe her own eyes. We grasped one another, looking at each other with silence and great astonishment, big tears rolling down her emaciated cheeks. A great number of people soon came together. She trembled as she held me by the hand and called me by the familiar names by which I well remember I used to be called by my grandmother, who has since died in slavery. We could not say much, but sat still, and cast now and then an affectionate look at each other—a look which violence and oppression had long checked— an affection which had nearly been extinguished by the long space of twenty-five years. My two sisters who were captured with us, are both with my mother, who takes care of them and her grandchildren in a small town not far from here, called Abàkà. Thus unsought for—after all search for me had failed— God has brought us together again, and turned our sorrow into joy.'

Shortly afterwards, during a tribal war, Abàkà was destroyed by the enemy, and Crowther's sisters, their husbands, and children sold as slaves. He however ransomed them; and his mother, safe in Abeokuta, became the first-fruits of the mission there. That it was blessed with success may be gathered by a note which Crowther makes in his journal, under date August 3rd, 1849: "This mission is to-day three years old. What has God wrought during this short interval of conflict between light and darkness! We have 500 constant attendants on the means

THE ROCK OF OLUMO, ABEOKUTA.

of grace, about 80 communicants, and nearly 200 candidates for baptism. A great number of heathen have ceased worshipping their country's gods; others have cast theirs away altogether, and are not far from enlisting under the banner of Christ."

About this time Mr. Townsend was recalled to England, and the Egba chiefs of their own accord, sent by him a letter to the Queen, expressing their gratitude for the repression of the slave trade, and asking that commerce might be encouraged with the Yoruba nation.

"We have seen your servants the missionaries; what they have done is agreeable to us. They have built a House of God. They have taught the people the Word of God and our children beside. We begin to understand them."

The Earl of Chichester was instructed to reply graciously to this native appeal; and on a grand occasion when all the great chiefs were gathered together for that purpose, on May 23rd, 1849, the answer was read. Mr. Crowther was the spokesman, and translated the letter sentence by sentence in their ears. Here is part of it.

"The Queen and people of England are very glad to know that Sagbua and the chiefs think as they do upon the subject of commerce. But commerce alone will not make a nation great and happy like England. England has been great and happy by the knowledge of the true God and Jesus Christ. The Queen is, therefore, very glad to hear that Sagbua and the chiefs have so kindly received the missionaries who carry with them the Word of God, and that so many people are willing to hear it."

With this kind and admirable message came some presents, two magnificent Bibles in English and Arabic respectively from the Queen, and a steel corn mill from Prince Albert; this latter was a marvel to the men. Crowther tells us how in their sight he fixed the mill; and then some Indian corn being put in the funnel, to their great astonishment it came out white flour by simply turning the handle. It is worthy of note that Crowther was a practical friend and helper to these people. He taught them handicrafts, and encouraged them in the cultivation of cotton, for which there seemed a wonderful opening in the way of trade.

The labours of these missionaries, and their friends at home, for the restriction, if not total suppression, of the slave trade, began to bear good fruit. The principal centre of this infamous traffic on the coast was Lagos, where, after vainly trying to impose pledges upon the slave-owning tyrant of the district, the English took possession of the place, and soon changed what had been a desolate swamp with the most distressing associations, into a thriving and prosperous town. Lagos became a commercial outlet of considerable importance, and a brisk trade was speedily established between this place and Liverpool.

Once more we find Crowther in England, and this time engaged with Lord Palmerston in placing before him the condition of things at Abeokuta, enlisting his sympathy and help for the native Christians. The king of Dahomey, with such a vile reputation for cruelty and bloodshed, was narassing the states which desired to co-operate with the English people in the advancement of religion and commerce. The words of Crowther were not unavailing, and Lord Palmerston soon afterwards wrote to him in the following words :

" I am glad to have an opportunity of thanking you again for the important and interesting information with regard to Abeokuta, which you communicated to me when I had the pleasure of seeing you at my house in August last. I request that you will assure your countrymen, that H.M. Government take a lively interest in the welfare of the Egba natives, and of the community settled at Abeokuta, which town seems destined to be a centre from which the lights of Christianity and of civilization may be spread over the neighbouring countries."

Supported by such a generous interest in the welfare of the people, the Missionary Societies in England stirred themselves to reach out to the natives of the interior the blessings of the Gospel ; and the Church Missionary Committee were not behindhand in the good cause.

Crowther, who was still working in England, was able to complete his valuable dictionary of the Yoruba language, for the service of out-going helpers; and the Rev. O. Vidal, a clergyman of remarkable linguistic gifts, was consecrated Bishop of Sierra Leone.

God's ways are past finding out, and it is lamentable to record that this faithful and useful pastor of the flock of Christ was spared only for two years, dying, to the regret and loss of all, on his way to England. But though the great Taskmaster buries his workers, the work goes on ; and as those whom He sent to feed

His flock on that fatal shore were in succession laid
low, He supplied their places with other brave and
capable men.

Although in Bishop Vidal the Mission lost a valuable helper the vacant episcopate was well filled again
by Bishop Weeks, who had a long and useful knowledge
of the colony already. Then on his decease from fever,
after two years' work, Dr. Bowen left the Holy Land
to take his place. Two years more, and he, too, died
in harness; and since then Sierra Leone has had
three other bishops in succession.

CHAPTER VII.

ANOTHER BRAVE AND BETTER VOYAGE.

———✳———

" Thou, whose Almighty Word,
Chaos and darkness heard,
    And took their flight,
Hear us, we humbly pray,
And where the Gospel-day
Sheds not its glorious ray
    Let there be light."—MARRIOTT.

———✳———

A N expedition was once more fitted out to learn the
secret of the Niger, and to follow—and if possible
further extend—the path of their unhappy predecessors.
In this case it was with the consent, but not at the
expense of the English Government, having been
started by Mr. Macgregor Laird, a merchant of Mincing
Lane, who, with a small party on his vessel the *Pleiad*,
had made up his mind " to establish a basis of commerce with the nations of the interior." There was
also another incentive in the fact that Dr. Barth, the
eminent African traveller, was supposed to be lost in
the interior, and it was hoped that the expedition
might meet with him, and bring him home. By the

permission of the Committee of the Church Missionary Society, Crowther was permitted to accompany the explorers, and Mr. Simon Jonas, a native interpreter and a Christian, was also allowed to make another of the party.

Crowther had by this time returned to Africa, and had continued, at Abeokuta and elsewhere, to make known the unsearchable riches of Christ. He spent some time in Sierra Leone, preaching in a manner to arouse the greatest enthusiasm on behalf of his work up the river. On landing at Lagos he was struck with the recollections of the place, when as a little slave boy he had first caught sight, with fear and trembling, of the great sea. He says, "I could well recollect many places I knew during my captivity, so I went over the spots where slave barracoons used to be. What a difference! Some of the spots are now converted into plantations of maize and cassava, and sheds built on others are filled with casks of palm oil and other merchandise, instead of slaves in chains and irons, in agony and despair."

His church at Abeokuta was a large and well-built edifice, boasting eight windows, and generally filled with a dense congregation of about three hundred natives. In one place the school children were seated, and all through the service the attentive audience, dressed in native costume, was a gratifying example of what Christianity can do for the welfare of savage man.

Already the babalamos or priests were gaining an ascendency over the mind of the new chief, and as a consequence a persecution broke out which sorely tried the faithfulness of the converts. At one time so

violent did this tyranny rage that Crowther's house
was watched day and night, and none suffered to
speak to the missionaries under pain of death.

Under such circumstances those who were stedfast
were brought into more vital union with each other
and their common Lord ; and when a better day dawned,
it was upon a church purified and established in faith
and patience. We can well imagine with what
affection and regret these simple people came to say
farewell to Crowther as once more he essayed to extend
the Kingdom of God into regions of the upper river
which they had not visited before.

His journals of this voyage are full of deep interest,
and extracts from them will be welcome to the reader
of these pages. When the party began to ascend the
river, with the dismal recollection of the death-rate
of the previous expedition in view, Crowther thought
that probably the mischief of fever which had been
so fatal then was the result of the green wood being
packed in the bunkers for days together, and therefore he suggested the advisability in this case of
stowing the fuel in canoes to drift astern. This pre-
caution, which was readily adopted, doubtless saved
the expedition from sickness and consequent failure.

On the 21st July 1854, the *Pleiad* anchored off Aboh
or Ibo, where the brave explorers of 1841 had made
some progress with the king. They had promised one
day to return, and it is said that the old man used to
watch in vain for the coming ships, and at last told
his sons with a sad regret, "The white man has
forgotten me and his promise too." There had also
been some misunderstanding about the death of Mr.
Carr, a medical missionary who had disappeared in

the king's dominions, and hostilities were actually commenced with a view to punish Obi for the offence. In Mr. Schön's opinion, however, the old king was innocent, and would have protected the Englishman had it been in his province and power. When the *Pleiad* reached the place, it was to hear of the old king's decease, and that his three sons were disputing the heirship, and indeed agreeing only upon the one point: that when the white man came he would tell them who should reign. The rightful heir seems to have been Tshukûma, and to him Crowther and his party paid a pre-arranged visit.

He says, "We landed close to Tshukûma's house, which was very small and confined, his old house had been lately burnt. He had been worshipping his god that morning, which we saw on his piazza, in a calabash placed in the front of a wall, covered with a white sheet. We waited about ten minutes before Tshukûma made his appearance, dressed in a pair of thin Turkish trousers, a white shirt, a white waistcoat, and a string of coral beads about his neck. He is smaller in size than Obi, his father, is very soft in his manners, and seems not possessed of much energy. He shook us all heartily by the hand, and in a short time the little square was crowded to excess, so that there was no room to move, and the place seemed so thronged that it was difficult to keep one's seat on the mat spread for our accommodation. Tshukûma used all his efforts to command silence, but to no purpose. Obi's daughters and the chief's wives took their turns to command silence, but it only increased the noise. At last Tshukûma requested us to frighten the people away, which of course we did not do. As it was impossible to obtain perfect silence, I suggested to Dr. Baikie to begin business, as we could manage to keep close enough to hear each other."

After this a conference was held, and an endeavour was made to remove the feeling of suspicion and want of confidence which rested on the mind of Tshukûma. "Even then," adds Crowther, "Tshukûma said my words were too good to hope that they would be realised, and that he would not believe anything until he had seen us do as we proposed; that there was no difficulty on their part, nor need we fear any unwillingness to receive those who may be sent to them, or learn what they may be taught; but that the fault rests with us, in not fulfilling what we promised to do." This will show how quick-witted these heathen are, and how jealous of their own importance.

Shortly afterwards the king came on board the vessel, where they had further conversation; and came again on Sunday, July 23rd, when Crowther preached on deck from the words, "Behold the Lamb of God, which taketh away the sin of the world." The service over, Crowther tells us that he hastened to go ashore in order to speak to the people in the town, and he then had the opportunity of a conversation with the chief on the all-important subject of religion—Simon Jonas interpreting as he went on.

This is how this royal savage received the message: " The quickness with which he caught my explanation of the all-sufficient sacrifice of Jesus Christ, the Son of God, for the sin of the world was gratifying. I endeavoured to illustrate it to him in this simple way, What would you think of any persons who in broad daylight like this, should light their lamps to assist the brilliant rays of the sun to enable them to see better? He said it would be useless, they would be fools to do so. I replied, Just so—that the sacrifice of Jesus Christ, the Son of God, was sufficient to take away our sins, just as one sun was sufficient to give light unto the whole world; that the worship of country fashion and numerous sacrifices, which shone like lamps only on account of the darkness of their ignorance and superstition, though repeated again and again, yet cannot take away our sins; but that the sacrifice of Jesus Christ, once offered, can alone take away the sin of the world. He frequently repeated the name, Oparra Tshuku! Oparra Tshuku!" (Son of God! Son of God!)

After varying experiences they reached Idda, and sent word they would pay the Atta, or chief thereof, a visit. Here, again, as in the expedition of 1841, the king refused to demean himself by going into a canoe to receive his guests; and it was not until after considerable delay they reached his place, and found him sitting outside the verandah of the palace, on a mud bank overspread with a cloth, with an old carpet at his feet. On the carpet were placed his royal message sticks, with brass bells attached to them, and an old broken Souter-Johnny jug stood before him. He had on a silk velvet tobi and a crown of white beads fringed with red parrot tails in front, with other fanciful decorations. His neck was covered with a large quantity of strung cowries and corals, and other beads. This interview showed the necessity for the diplomatic tact with which Crowther, in dealing with these chiefs, prevented disagreeable results.

As they proceeded up the river, traces were continually seen of the ravages committed by the Filatas, who appeared to be organized bandits, unwilling to work themselves, and living upon the fruits of the industry of others. So terrible was the desolation wrought by Dasaba, one of the chiefs, that the whole of the right bank of the Niger had been cleared of every town and village to the number of about a hundred, and the inhabitants sold into slavery or killed.

An example of the practice of these bloodthirsty tribes is furnished in the words of Crowther's journal on August 11th. He tells us, "In the afternoon he landed at Kende, where some of the few who escaped seizure by the Filatas at Pandu have taken refuge. Here again is a picture of the misery these poor people are doomed to go through, for they live destitute of everything but their liberty, and that with difficulty. The Filatas, whose aim is not so much to kill as to seize and enslave, took Pandu by treachery. They professed friendship, and entered the town on that pretence, and the king presented them with bullocks and other necessaries. But when a sufficient number had got in, they commenced seizing the inhabitants, and scarcely gave them time to make resistance. Only the king, Oyigu, and a few persons about him, made any effort to repel them; but the

CROWTHER ADDRESSING THE AFRICAN KING TSHUKUMA.

king could not long stand against his enemies, and was killed in the attempt. A great number was caught, and very few were so fortunate as to escape. The neighbouring towns and villages were immediately deserted by the inhabitants, who took refuge on the left side of the river."

It is not surprising that the appearance of the white men struck terror into the minds of the poor natives, who had lost all hope and happiness under the rule of these Filatas. When the steamer had reached Oruko the passage had become increasingly intricate, and the shallows were very dangerous to their progress. At last the captain, with Dr. Hutchinson and Mr. Guthrie, got into a boat to take soundings, and returned with the decision not to proceed any further. However, Dr. Baikie, who was, with Crowther, exceedingly anxious to penetrate these unknown regions, took entire charge of the vessel, and reached a place where Adama, the king of the Bassa country, met him. This king had also the same sad story to tell of the devastation of the country by the slave trade; and after receiving a few presents, undertook to protect any white men who should come up the river. The old man, who was of small stature, was elaborately prepared for the visit, having on a patchwork shirt of blue and white triangles, and a red Turkey cap on his head. He exhibited considerable politeness to his guest, and they observed that he was saluted by kneeling on the ground, two fingers of each hand being rubbed in the dust, which is then rubbed on the forehead several times. The people salute each other by embracing, the right hand being stretched parallel with the other as far as the shoulder.

On more than one occasion the explorers were in considerable danger. Crowther tells us that at one time they started for the Mitchi market to purchase yams and other food. " On our approach we heard a great noise and clamour in the market, which is held in canoes on the water side, and when we came near, all the Ojgo canoes had dispersed in different directions, and everything was in great confusion. Some of the women were crying, for the Mitchis had plundered their property, and a strong party had armed themselves with bows and poisoned arrows to oppose our landing. We were but a few yards from them, but could not speak directly with them ; besides which there was such uproar and excitement that it was impossible to gain their attention. They at times beckoned us in defiance to land, and armed people were stationed along the bank to oppose our doing so. There was not a single weapon in our boat. Dr. Baikie held out some handkerchiefs as an inducement, but the very sight of them seemed to enrage the people. At last an old grey-bearded man, who seemed to be the chief, with great passion and significant motion of both hands, wished us away."

The visitors wisely followed this advice. They afterwards found that these warlike natives were cannibals, who devoured the bodies of their enemies killed in battle. Still, it is very satisfactory to note that in most cases the people received these visits kindly, and showed their gratitude to the white man for coming to restore peace to their country.

Once a singular expression was used by a native whom they descried on the bank of the river. They addressed him in the Haussa language, which he evidently understood, and told him they had come from the white man's country, and wanted to see the chief. Immediately he shouted, "Bature Anasara maidukia na gode alla;" that is, "White men, the Nazarenes, men of property, I thank God." Still repeating this strange cry, he assisted the party to land, and led them into the bush, where the chief and a large party of armed warriors gave them a cordial reception. Perfectly defenceless, the white men moved safely among them, and delighted the chief and some of his headmen by shaking hands with them.

Crowther draws attention here to the mistake which explorers make in judging the natives of Africa as always hostile to Europeans. Making allowance for the antipathy aroused everywhere by the slave trade, and bearing in mind that the frequent tribal wars made the carrying of arms almost a necessity, he is still of opinion that where once an Englishman's peaceful intentions have been made clear, he has no cause to be afraid.

On the 7th November the gallant explorers safely reached Fernando Pó, and heartily joined in raising their Ebenezer of thanksgiving for journeying mercies, through many perils and hardships without a single person being the worse either from sickness or accident. Such a four months' experience led Crowther to close his journal with the words, " May this singular instance of God's favour and protection drive us nearer to the Throne of grace, to humble ourselves before our God, whose instrument we are, and who can continue or dispense with our services as it seems good to His unerring wisdom."

CHAPTER VIII.

A VOYAGE AND A WRECK.

———⁂———

" Speed Thy servants, Saviour, speed them,
   Thou art Lord of winds and waves ;
They were bound, but Thou hast freed them,
   Now they go to free the slaves ;
      Be Thou with them,
'Tis Thine arm alone that saves."—KELLY.

———⁂———

A GREAT advance had been made. It was clear that
the Niger was navigable, and that the natives
were not unwilling to receive the representatives of
the Christian faith. Crowther returned to Abeokuta,
and having had a conference with Mr. and Mrs.
Hinderer at Ibadan, and Mr. Mann at Ijaye, the
plan of missionary effort in the Yoruba country and
elsewhere was fully discussed.

Soon afterwards Mr. Göllmer, who had been his
coadjutor in establishing the Christian church at
Abeokuta, returned to Europe, and Crowther was
compelled to take his place at Lagos, with the super-
vision of the mission stations on the coast. Here he
laboured hard at his translation of the Bible into the

Yoruba language, and also prepared a primer, a vocabulary, and several extracts from the Word of God in the Ibo language.

In the year 1856 his old teacher and guardian, Mr. Weeks, returned to Africa, as we have already mentioned, as Bishop of Sierra Leone. After a very profitable visitation of the mission field up the river, he fell ill, and to the grief of all, and especially of Crowther, died at Sierra Leone.

The time had now arrived when in the judgment of the Church Missionary Society another expedition should be arranged to establish a Niger Christian Mission. The Committee made an appeal by deputation to Lord Palmerston, and in 1857 the *Dayspring* started on her way. It was at first intended that six different stations were to be established as the basis of future mission work, and for this purpose half-a-dozen native ministers were to accompany Mr. Crowther and his fellow European missionaries. This, however, was not to be ; Bishop Weeks died, as we have seen, and with him passed to his rest, Mr. Frey, one of the hard-working ministers of his diocese. Another heavy loss was occasioned by the death of Mr. Beale, one of the mission staff who had conferred with Crowther about the approaching expedition of the *Dayspring*. Thus the mission work at Sierra Leone was unable to spare the native teachers originally allotted to the work, and the vessel had to start with Crowther, a native pastor, Rev. J. C. Taylor, from Ibo, Crowther's old friend Simon Jonas, and two youths who had been residing with Mr. Schön. Of all the expeditions this was, humanly speaking, the least prepared for such a great and difficult enterprise, and yet it was from the *Dayspring* that the first stations were planted of the Niger mission. The importance of this journey up the river cannot be over-estimated; and although it came to an abrupt termination at Rabbah, we shall find its record, as described in Crowther's journal, full of interest.

One of the principal features of the new plan of campaign was to establish a strong station at Abo, where the old king Obi, as we have already seen, showed such a willingness to receive the European guests. They had already on a previous occasion visited Tshukûma, who was favourably disposed towards the mission, but now they made the acquaintance of Aje, his brother, and certainly the impression of him was not happy. When invited on board he demanded rum, and was evidently chiefly disposed to lay his hand upon whatever he could get. He appears to have been a fine example of the acquisitive heathen. Much of his impertinence and bad manners Crowther charitably attributes to his familiarity with Europeans from an early age. Common honesty was clearly not one of his virtues, for he successfully purloined, or attempted to do so, Crowther's slippers, the dinner bell, the cushion against which his royalty leaned, and a cigar which one of the party incautiously held in his hand during the interview.

When the party landed, and prepared to secure a piece of ground for premises of the mission, with the joint consent of these two rival dignities, Aje was furiously jealous of Tshukûma's presents, and was finally pacified with a pink cocked hat, and umbrella of a like gaudy hue. Poor human nature! Subsequently Aje, with all his wives dressed in ships' bunting, tried to make an impression of his greatness, and what was much more serious, opposed and interfered with the establishment of the mission in his country. And yet Crowther makes this fair note of this individual on leaving him. "Before quitting Abo for the present I think it is right and just to say a word in favour of Aje's faithfulness in one respect, whatever his failings may be in other matters. It will be remembered that through an interposition in 1854, the prisoners who were confined and would have been either killed or sold for their offences, were then released. Since that time they have never been touched, and really pardoned, according to Aje's promise to us. One of these men on seeing me, fell on his knees in thankfulness for his deliverance, and on the return of his companions, who had been absent, they brought me some palm wine as an acknowledgment of their gratitude. Had not these men introduced themselves three years after it might have been doubted whether Aje had fulfilled his promise."

Leaving this place, the *Dayspring* passed on to a very important town, Onitsha, which is 140 miles up the river, and on Ibo territory. At first, in alarm at the first sight of white men and their ships, the natives appeared with their weapons in their hands; but they were soon reassured, and led the party along a road to their town.

The cotton, yams, and Indian corn were very well cultivated, and the conduct of the king Akazua and his headmen showed no small amount of intelligence. The visitors were entertained by the king and his councillors, who heard with respect all their proposed plans; and, after a conference together, the king stepped forth and appealed to the people whether they agreed to them or not. A spot was agreed upon where the Mission buildings could be erected, and a hired house was taken in preparation for a factory. The town itself is embosomed in trees, and pleasantly situated; and the houses are arranged in twenty-six groups. Each comprised about 250 persons, so the population as a whole is not far short of 6500 souls. Here, however, they were in fear of their enemies, and to prevent a surprise have look-out posts established in high trees, where a constant vigilance is displayed.

One day, when the visitors entered the place, there was great rejoicing, beating of drums, dancing and frantic gestures and moving. Crowther says, "When we came to our lodging, one of the headmen paid us a visit, and I asked him the cause of this amusement, and was told it was in honour of the burial of a relative of our landlord who died some six months ago. Simon Jonas, who remained on shore last night, had heard that a human sacrifice was to be made to the manes of the dead, and he told the people of the wickedness of the practice. On my putting the question as to the cause of the amusement, the headman was conscience stricken, and told Simon Jonas that the victim was not yet killed. We then took the opportunity, and spoke most seriously to the headman in the hearing of many people, who stood in the square, of the abomination of this wicked practice, the more so, as the victim was a poor, blameless, female slave. He then assured us that he had not known that it was wrong to do so; but as we had now told them, the human sacrifice should not be performed, but a bullock should be killed in its stead. He proposed that we should buy the woman, that they might buy a bullock with the cowries in her stead. This we refused to do, as we are not slave traders. He then said that the woman should be sold to somebody else, which we thought was better than to kill her. Before we returned to the ship, Simon Jonas was told that the poor woman was loosed from her bonds."

Here Crowther left Mr. Taylor to prepare the work and settle the mission at Onitsha.

We follow the voyagers through various experiences until they reach Idda. Here, after much delay and parade of heathen dignity, the party were admitted to the Atta, who received them in great state, seated on his throne and dressed in a rich silk-velvet robe of light green hue. The conference was much assisted by the presence and sympathy of the Lady Adama, a dowager queen, and a site for mission buildings was secured in a very favourable situation. The position of this town, standing on a high cliff, and overlooking the confluence of the Kworra and Tshadda rivers, marked it as a point of great value in the future plan of work.

Passing up the Kworra the *Dayspring* soon found itself on the friendly waters of the Galadima, and here they were shown an old copy of the Koran. The importance of a knowledge of Arabic was evident; and Crowther makes a note at this point, that their native catechists should be taught this language at the seminary at Sierra Leone. He tells us how in the town of Gbebe he began teaching the natives :—

"Besides my English, I took an Arabic Bible and

Schön's translations of Matthew and John into Haussa, and an Ibo primer, out of which to teach the alphabet. Taking my seat in the Galadima's ante-hall—which is the common resort of all people, holding from forty to fifty persons—a number of both sexes, old and young, soon entered as usual to look on. Having carefully placed my books on the mat, after the custom of the Mallams, Mr. Crooke sitting on my right, and Kasumo on my left, I commenced my conversation by telling them that to-day was the Christian Sabbath, in which we rest from our labour, according to the commandment of God. The Galadima came in, and to him I read some verses from the third chapter of St. John in the Haussa language, in the hearing of the people, which he understood, and which by further explanation became more intelligible to him. In the meantime some Mohammedans walked in, and desired to see the Arabic Bible, which I delivered to Kasumo to read and translate to them. The Galadima, who reads Arabic, expressed a wish, as soon as the school is opened, to learn to read Haussa in Roman or Italic character. There was an intelligent young man present who could read Arabic, who was also very anxious to read our translations in the Italic character.

"After a long talk I ran over the alphabet from the Ibo primer several times, with the Galadima and the young man, at which they showed much quickness and intelligence. I then gave this Arabic copy of the Bible as a present to the Galadima. This was so unexpected that he did not know how sufficiently to express his gratitude in words, and, contrary to the usage of the Mohammedans, he actually was going to throw dust on his forehead, as a token of the value he placed on the gift, when Kasumo stopped him by saying it was not our custom to do so. He said his father would be able to read it fluently. May the Lord bless this small and feeble beginning of an attempt to introduce the religion of Christ into this benighted part of Africa! May the prayers of the Church be heard on its behalf."

We shall see later on that this prayer was answered.

At Egga or Eggan, as it is there pronounced, they found an aged chief who remembered the 1841 Expedition, and received them very cordially. His town is filthy, and after a shower of rain almost impassable with soft mud. His Majesty used high clogs under the circumstances; while his guests, sinking at every step far above the ankles, panted after him in vain. Picking their way through the streets they heard a little boy rehearsing his lesson in Arabic; and further on, seeing what they thought to be a mosque, they found a barber's shop, in which the operators were shaving the head, the eyebrows, the armpits, and the nostrils of their customers with marvellous facility and safety.

As they passed Fo-Fo, the mate of the *Dayspring* breathed his last, and was buried on the sand beach. Arriving at Rabbah the *Dayspring* unhappily struck upon a rock, and within a very short time settled down aft on her starboard side. Crowther and his companions escaped in time upon the shore; and under the discomfort of a severe tornado made a tent of mats, into which they gathered such effects as they could rescue, and began to look very anxiously for the

WRECK OF THE " DAYSPRING " ON THE ROCKS AT RABHAH.

steamer *Sunbeam*, which was to follow them. To add to the danger of the situation, the native Kroomen were insubordinate, and the headman had to be threatened with irons to save a revolt.

The native chiefs into whose hands they had fallen were not very friendly; and in addition to the disappointment occasioned by the loss of the ship and the termination of the enterprise, they had much to unsettle and distress them. But one day, in the midst of a crowd of warriors, a strange voice saluted them with, "Good morning, sir!" and the speaker proved to be Henry George, a Sunday scholar at Abeokuta who had joined the army of Dasaba, and had passed through many trials. This providential meeting led to the man being engaged by Crowther as guide and servant, and he accompanied them on their overland journey to Abeokuta.

Reaching Ogbomosho they were delighted to meet with the Rev. Mr. Clark, a Baptist minister, who entertained them. Shortly afterwards they spent Christmas Day on the banks of the Niger, one of the party concocting a plum pudding. After a narrow escape from the attack of a leopard, and other stirring incidents, they had the melancholy duty of burying Mr. Howard, the purser, and one of the Kroomen, who had died.

At one time they were passing through a Mohammedan district at the time of the Ramadan, and much conversation ensued upon the observation of the Christian Sabbath and the obligation of fasting. "Do not the Anasaras fast?" was a constant query. Crowther's reply was, "Yes, they do fast; but the fast of the Anasaras is of a more private and conscientious kind than your public one. Thousands of the Anasaras may fast to-day, and their neighbours know nothing of it; but their fast is known only to God and themselves. Just so is their prayer in secret, as Christ has taught us!" The reply always received was, "You are true persons; and your religion is superior to ours."

It is noticeable how frequently these poor heathen expressed their appreciation of the advantage of the Christian religion as compared with their own, even when mixed with those inducements which to the natural man would be so attractive in the creed of Mohammed. The truth is, in the Gospel of the Lord Jesus Christ they heard the voice of a herald proclaiming good news of liberty to the captive, not merely as regards slavery, but with respect to those galling bonds which a false religion had thrust upon them. They had endured a yoke, but had never known a peace; and to them at last came One who bade them come unto Him in their weariness, and He would give them refreshment of soul and rest.

An Enforced Halt—Onitsha.

———✳———

"Come labour on !
Away with gloomy doubts and faithless fear,
No arm so weak but may do service here ;
By feeblest agents can our God fulfil
    His righteous will.

"Come labour on !
No time for rest, till glows the western sky,
While the long shadows o'er our pathway lie,
And a glad sound comes with the setting sun,
    Servants, well done !"—H. L. L.

———✳———

THE loss of the *Dayspring*, while it precluded any further progress up the river, left Crowther and his party to settle for a time at Rabbah and the immediate neighbourhood.   That which is perplexing to the human mind is, however, always in God's good time evidence of His goodwill and guiding providence ; and so we find that the visits of the future Bishop of the Niger to the kings and headmen of these out-of-the-way places prepared the way for the establishment of Christian missions in their midst at a future day.

Crowther's journals, written in the midst of these

wild people, and often under circumstances of peril, are full of deeply interesting incidents. The people of Nupé held the great river which flowed through their land, the Niger, in high esteem. Their intensely superstitious minds had believed it to be the mother of all the rivers of the world, and it was customary when the corn ripened to offer a few grains to the rushing stream, with many prayers to propitiate its powers. Here also there is the divine worship of the manes of the dead which we find in all quarters of the inhabited world. That strange undying impress of immortality links the living with those who are passed into the land of spirits.

As in Yoruba, the natives of Nupé sacrifice to these spirits under the personation of a mask, and Crowther tells us that the Gunuko or masquerader who performs this function is of an enormous height. Raised some twelve or fifteen feet by slight bamboo supports, and dressed in a frightful costume, he dances along the villages, filling the hearts of the people with terror, and his own hands with the cowries which they gladly give him.

This constant fear, which made the hearts of the poor natives quake, was prevalent everywhere, and Crowther laboured hard to break the fetter from their spirits, pointing them to that Great Deliverer whose perfect love casteth out all fear.

In one respect the religion of the Yoruba natives corresponds with that of the Chinese. They have a rite by which a sheep is offered as a sacrifice to their ancestors. In our illustration the figures traced on the wall represent the honoured dead, and the various

birds, agricultural implements, and so forth, are to
set forth his rank and condition. The zigzag scroll
work is the sacred signs of the Oro worship, and is
coloured red and white. Before the victim is killed
some leaves are given to it; and when its blood is
shed it is caught in a bowl, and then reverently
sprinkled upon the forehead of the persons present.

During Crowther's wanderings at this time the work
and influence of Mohammedanism was plainly dis-
cerned as having its iron grip on the consciences of
the people; and when in the course of his preaching
he alluded to Adam, Noah, Abraham, or any of the
ancient patriarchs, the natives recognised the names
at once as being taught them by the Mallams.

These teachers of the false prophet are most diligent
in their efforts to extend the belief of their religion.
Sometimes they will spend the whole night in the
tents of the kings and chiefs, reading to them from
the Koran, and expounding it to their listeners. Its
strange and imaginative stories, just written in a style
to catch the attention of a barbaric outlaw, with his
many wives and unlimited lust of battle, chain the
attention of the African people.

In the practical working of the Moslem creed, too, the
harms and fetishes are found very useful auxiliaries,
as, for instance, when the story of Jonah is told. The
Mallams relate that this prophet, called Nunsa-bun-
Mata (Jonah the son of Amittai), presumptuously flinging himself into the sea, a great fish swallowed him.
An alligator then swallowed the fish; and finally a
hippopotamus swallowed the alligator. So in these
threefold walls Jonah hid a thousand years, and then
in answer to his prayer God commanded these creatures

SACRIFICIAL WORSHIP OF ANCESTORS AMONG THE NATIVES.

to throw him upon the land. The gaping wonder
with which this extraordinary story is received may
be well imagined; and the lesson is so readily believed
that whenever anyone has a fish-bone in his throat he
has only to say "Nunsa-bun-Mata," and the charm
will remove it. ·

Crowther on several occasions saw these Mallams
produce a long parchment roll inscribed with the
names of the great angels and prophets, beginning
with Gabriel, and at the foot of the list is Isa, Jesus.

Surely the day will come, is the anticipation of the
true Christian, when He whose right it is to reign,
whose Name is above every name, shall enlighten
these dark places of the earth with His glorious light
of life.   Crowther, face to face with this great enemy
of Christianity, places on record his impressions of
the magnitude of the evil, and how needful it is that
Mohammedanism shall be dealt with wisely.   He
says :—

"These are the people Christian missionaries have
to withstand and oppose ; their false doctrines have to
be exposed, their errors corrected, and they, as well as
the heathen population, led and directed to Him who
is 'the Way, the Truth, and the Life.'   In doing this
a few things must be remembered, namely, that they
are the *masters* of the country, and bigoted protectors
of their religion, and that by this 'craft' the Mallams
have their wealth.   If these things are not well pon-
dered, and the instruction of our blessed Saviour, 'Be
wise as serpents,' is not closely adhered to and
practised, we may defeat our object of doing any good,
either to the Mohammedans themselves or to the
heathen population under their government.   Now

that so many centuries have passed without this light of the glorious Gospel of Christ shining into the country, and into the dark hearts of this benighted people, now that it has pleased the Lord of the harvest to give the Church an access to them, shall His servants by an unwise step block up the way against themselves, and the introduction of the Gospel of Christ, by a zeal without knowledge, which may prompt them to act as if the natives were the nation to be converted in a day?

" The soil on which we have to work in this un-ploughed ground is gross heathenism and Moham-medan bigotry, through ignorance.

" The Word preached finds a more yielding soil in the minds of the heathen hearers than in that of prejudiced Mohammedans. The same reasonable Scriptural exposure of the heathen superstition made use of by the Prophet Elijah (1 Kings xviii.), by the Psalmist (Psa. cxv.), and by the Prophet Isaiah (lxiv.), sympathetically read to them, applied to the hearts by the Holy Spirit, never failed to have the desired effect. Hence our success among this class of the people, among whom we labour.

" On the contrary, Mohammedanism arms the hearts of its professors with deadly weapons against Chris-tianity, by denying its fundamental doctrine, the Sonship of Christ, and His divinity as one with God the Father, to be blasphemy according to the teaching of the Koran.

" Thus their hearts are hardened with prejudices, self-conceit, self-righteous spirit, and self-confidence in their meritorious religious performances, especially in prayer and fasting, and in works of supererogation,

which they believe they can make over for the benefit
of others who are deficient. They are freely allowed
the indulgence of the sinful lust of the flesh; they do
not scruple to commit acts of cruelty and oppression
on those who are not professors of their faith; slave-
holding and trading is fully sanctioned, to carry out
which slave wars are waged against the heathens with
great cruelty, in order to enslave them with oppression
and violence, without remorse, contrary to the law of
charity, 'Do to others as you would that they should
do to you.' Hence slave wars have desolated the
lands of populous heathen tribes and nations, whose
inhabitants were carried away captives and sold into
slavery, and those who are reserved in the country are
doomed to perpetual servitude, hewers of wood and
drawers of water, and most oppressive tributaries.

"This is a faint description of the soil of the minds
of the professors of Islamism, in which the seed of the
Gospel of Jesus Christ is being attempted to be sown,
by preaching repentance of sin and a renewed change
of heart through faith in Christ Jesus the Son of God,
who is 'the Way, the Truth, and the Life,' without
whom none can come unto the Father. But for all his
earnestness, the preacher is looked upon with horrified
contempt as a blasphemer, because God never had a
Son. 'There is no God but God, and Mohammed is
His prophet.' Notwithstanding these stern oppositions
from Mohammedans, one feature of encouragement
that Christianity shall prevail must not be overlooked,
namely, Christianity was only recently introduced
into these parts of West Africa—to Abeokuta in the
Yoruba Mission in 1846, and to the Niger in 1857—
notwithstanding that Mohammedanism had been

introduced into these countries a century before, with full licence of all sinful enjoyments.

" What surprises me most is, that Christianity, with its strict restraints of the enjoyment of sinful lusts, and, moreover, enjoining conscientious self-denial of all the allurements of the world, the flesh, and the devil, should get so many converts in the face of all the free allowances in the enjoyments of all these by the religion of the false prophet. It proves that Christianity appeals to the hearts and consciences of man as a reasonable being who ought to judge between truth and error. Even some Mohammedans have been known to admit the truth of Christianity, but dare not confess it, lest they should be persecuted by their co-religionists. Notwithstanding all oppositions, Christ 'shall divide the spoil with the strong' in this spiritual warfare."

Crowther's idea clearly is that, instead of spending our time and strength in fighting the Moslem creed. we had better pass it by in silence, and trust to the sword of the Spirit to win the victory for Christ. Mohammedanism, baleful as it is, must be treated as an accomplished fact, which however must fade and lessen as the knowledge of the Saviour spreads abroad. But a positive attack upon it will probably result in the incensed enmity of its votaries, and the Christian missionaries being driven from the spheres of their labours for the Lord.

One of the most important results of the voyage of the *Dayspring* was the foundation being laid of the mission work at Onitsha. This important point on the Niger was reached at the end of July, 1857, and it will be remembered how favourably the visitors were received by the king, Obi Akazua. After Crowther had carefully prepared the way, and stayed for a short time to arrange with the king and his chiefs as to the site for mission premises, he left the Rev. J. C. Taylor, a native missionary, with Simon Jonas, the interpreter, to take charge of the work.

Fortunately, Mr. Taylor kept a journal of his experiences in the midst of this field of labour. He tells us that soon after he had settled down, he called upon one of the chiefs and entered into conversation with him in his hut. "I drew his mind to the principles of religion, and pointed out to him the sinful nature of man by nature. I asked him whether he had a soul? 'Yes,' he replied. 'How is that soul to be saved?' '*Amazoru*,' i.e., 'I do not know,' was the answer. Then I pointed out to him that Jesus Christ is 'the Way, the Truth, and the Life.' He exclaimed, '*Jesu Opara Tshuku, Zim uzo oma*,' i.e., 'Jesus, Son of God, show me the good way.'"

A difference arose with the king of Ogidi, and the missionary had to transfer his work to the war camp, and there he preached the Gospel with great effect. The Lord's Prayer, which he had translated into their tongue, made a deep impression upon them, the sentence of all others which seemed to strike them most being, "But deliver us from evil." As Mr. Taylor reasoned with them their faces assumed a wonderful change, and, from what he gathered, their faith in the false gods and fetishes was severely shaken. So gracious were the signs of success that he writes with great joy and earnestness: "I am thankful to say that I begin to see signs of the remarks of the late Bishop Vidal being fulfilled:

that the time will come when the Tshuku (gods) of
Abo and the Ibos in general shall fall down before
the Gospel, as Dagon fell before the ark. Their mul-
tifarious shrines shall give way for the full liberation
and introduction of the Gospel to their forlorn,
degraded, long bewitched, but ransomed people, to
lead them to God."

On every hand he found the people willing and
glad to hear the Gospel. On the morning of Sunday,
October 25th, a service was held in one of the
enclosed spaces near a chief's house, and a large
crowd of natives listened with eagerness to the Word
of God. Mr. Radillo, a Baptist interpreter, translated for Mr. Taylor, who, although very weak
through an attack of fever, preached a sermon on
the text from St. Luke: "If any man will come
after Me, let him deny himself, and take up his cross
daily and follow Me."

As the weary missionary was going home after the
service two women came to him, saying, "The word
is a true word, we will not be ashamed of Tshuku
(God). You must bear patiently till God shall turn
the whole of Onitsha to follow your religion, which
is far better than all our fetish customs." What a
wonderful word of encouragement from these poor
natives !

Mr. Taylor, in exchange, gave them also a loving
and cheering message from his Master, and urged
them both to follow the gracious Saviour whose word
they had heard that day. "One of them raised her
eyes unto heaven," he says, "and with uplifted hands
heaved out this short petition, 'Opara Tshuku mere
ayi ebere,' i.e., 'Son of God, have mercy upon me !'

Christians, imagine my feelings on this occasion. Might not the words of our Saviour be applied to her, 'Ought not this woman, being a daughter of Abraham, whom Satan hath bound these many years, be loosed from her bonds on the Sabbath day?'"

Still there was much to shock and distress the heart of the Christian in the conduct of these poor heathen. One day the missionary was walking with others towards the river, and presently a crowd shouting and crying approached them, dragging a poor young girl, tied hand and foot, with her face on the ground, to the river. This was one of the superstitious customs, for they believe in making a sacrifice for their sins by beating out the life of a fellow-creature in this manner. As she is drawn along, the crowd cry, "Aro ye, Aro, Aro!" *i.e.*, "Wickedness, wickedness!" and believe that the iniquities of the people are thus atoned for.

There is also a horrible practice among the Onitsha people of killing all children who happen to be born twins. This superstition is so deeply rooted that the mother is also degraded and cruelly treated. One such, a convert to Christianity, one night became the mother of two little girls, and immediately in sheer terror she fled to the bush for safety. Her friends hesitated about casting the infants away to be torn of wild beasts, as was customary, and sent for Mr. Perry, the minister. He said at once, "Destroy them not, for a blessing is on them;" and in spite of a perfect tumult of anger, "a furious mob of five hundred men armed to the teeth with guns, cutlasses, spears, clubs, bows and arrows, who surrounded the mission compound, demanding that the babes be given up to them," the little ones were safely conveyed to the English ship *Wanderer* on the Niger, and saved from destruction.

There is a celebrated god called Tshi, whose power is to preserve the people from witchcraft, and once, when visiting one of the chiefs, the visitors were asked by his wife to witness her sacrifice to this deity. A goat was killed, and the blood allowed to run into a bowl, and then over the slain victim, she said, "I beseech thee, my guide, make me good; thou hast life. I beseech thee to intercede with God the Spirit, tell Him my heart is clean. I beseech thee to deliver me from all bad thoughts in my heart; drive out all witchcrafts; let riches come to me. See your sacrificed goat; see your kotu-nuts; see your rum and palm wine." She tried to persuade her guests to drink some of this wine, but they refused.

To the great sorrow of Crowther and Mr. Taylor, on the return of the latter to Fernando Po, at the end of November, the sickness of Simon Jonas increased, and at last this useful helper in the mission work passed away. He was a great loss, not only for his excellent and consistent Christian character, but because of his ability in translating into the language of the tribes. On the Sunday after his death, Mr. Taylor records in his diary the following affecting incident :

"This morning a woman came into my residence and requested me to follow her, for she wanted to see me very particularly. I got myself ready and went with her. After walking about two miles we came to a very beautiful sand beach, where to my surprise I found twenty-four persons, well clad in decent dress, being twenty women and four men. One of them rose up and said, ‘Sir, we expressly sent for you to preach to us the Word of God; do, for we thirst to hear God’s living word; please, sir, help us!’ I stood under a hollow tree, and told them I was sorry I had no book with me. To my great surprise each one brought out a hymn book. I then gave out that beautiful hymn, ‘Jesus, where’er Thy people meet;’ and I took one of their Bibles, and expounded the words of the Apostle Paul from Acts xvi. 13: ‘And on the Sabbath we went out of the city by a riverside, where prayer was wont to be made; and we sat down, and spake unto the women which resorted thither.’ Thank God for this opportunity!”

CHAPTER X.

THE BOY BECOMES THE BISHOP.

————✳————

_ " Word of Life, most pure and strong,
    Lo ! for thee the nations long,
    Spread, till from its dreary night
    All the world awakes to light.

" Up the ripening fields you see,
    Mighty shall the harvest be,
    But the reapers still are few,
    Great the work they have to do."--BAHNMAIER.

————✳————

WE must now pass more rapidly in review the events of the next few years, in order to bring the narrative of Bishop Crowther's career up to the work in our own day.

In the closing months of 1858 we find Crowther once more starting from Onitsha for a canoe expedition up the river ; and after travelling thus over three hundred miles, he reached Rabbah in safety, the place of his enforced stay after the wreck of the _Dayspring_. From this point he made his way across country to Ilorin, the Haussa capital in his native country, and Abeokuta, the famous city under the stone; and from thence he proceeded to the coast, arriving at Lagos in the early part of the year 1859. The work, however, was destined to receive some opposition ; and the trial of faith which meets all true labourers in the vineyard of God was to prove Crowther and his companions.

From Rabbah, where he had laboured so hard to prepare the way for a mission establishment, there came bad news during that year. The *Rainbow* passing up the river was informed by Dr. Baikie that the place was no longer open to Christian work, and as a proof of the hostility of the natives, the ship on its return journey was attacked, and two of its crew lost their lives.

For a time it seemed as though the work of toilsome years was to be undone, and the workers, baffled at every point, must retire to the mouth of the river to await another opening. But danger and disappointment brings a true Christian to his knees, and so feeling his utter helplessness and incapacity, he is strengthened and comforted by all the fulness of God. He whose work it is will in due time, if we faint not, open a way through which we may go up and possess the land.

Mr. Taylor came to England, and awakened a new interest in the Niger work, and returning, he, in conjunction with Crowther, established an important mission at Akassa, the mouth of the Nun river, which is the navigable entrance to the Niger. When the gunboat *Espoir* ascended the river to effect reprisals upon the natives for their hostility to our vessels, Crowther was on board, and was thus able to visit some of the stations, to their great encouragement and advantage.

It was just at this time that Mr. Laird, to whose energy and enterprise so much of the Niger exploration was due, died, and as a result his factories on the river were closed. This was a great loss to the mission, and rendered their work increasingly difficult. Still a new hope dawned in the hearts of the missionaries when the *Investigator*, a vessel fully equipped for exploring the rivers, took Crowther and a number of helpers on board on its way. Once more they reached Onitsha, leaving Mr. Taylor to resume his old work. Here we are told Crowther found no less than twenty-eight natives ready for baptism, and the services of the mission church were attended by a large number of people.

Passing on to the confluence, he revisited his old station at Gbebe, and to his joy found that although for this long interval the people had been under the care of a single native catechist, the work of the Lord had prospered, and with a full heart Crowther baptized a number of those who had believed to salvation. He tells us, "This day at the morning service, though with fear and trembling, yet by faith in Christ, the great Head of the Church, who has commanded, 'Go ye, therefore, and teach all nations, baptizing them in the name of the Father, and of the Son, and of the Holy Ghost,' I took courage and baptized eight adults and one infant in our mud chapel, in the presence of a congregation of 192 persons, who all sat still with their mouths open in wonder and amazement, at the initiation of some of their friends and companions into a new religion by a singular rite, the form in the name of the Trinity being translated into Nupé, and distinctly pronounced as each candidate knelt. These nine persons are the first-fruits of the Niger mission. Is not this a token of the Lord to the Society to persevere in the arduous work to introduce Christianity among the vast populations on the bank of the Niger, and that they shall reap in due time if they faint not? More so when the few baptized persons represent several tribes of large tracts of countries on the banks of the Niger, Tshadda, Igara, Igbira, Gbari Eki, or Burnu, and even a scattered Yoruba was among them. Is not this an anticipation of the immense fields opened to the Church to occupy for Christ?"

The sunshine of a great prosperity came upon Crowther and his work, and with unremitting energy he passed hither and thither along the banks of the Niger, establishing at different points fresh centres of Christian enlightenment. Neither was he wanting in helping these poor heathen to help themselves by promoting commerce; his practical and business abilities prepared quite a market for the cotton trade in the district. He was anxious to show them that the Christians came to them with a message of peace and goodwill, and that the introduction of the cotton manufacture in the mission premises was to their advantage.

On one occasion king Masaba, of Nupé, sent to Crowther messengers, and these he conducted round his mission buildings at Gbebe, showing them the goods and their preparations for shipment to the white man's country. This is the message he sent back to the king: "We are Anasera (Nazarenes); *there* (pointing to the schoolroom) we teach the Christian religion; *these* (pointing to the cotton gins

PALACE OF THE KING OF YORUBA, AND RECEPTION OF MISSIONARIES BY HIS MAJESTY. [p. 115.

I

are our guns; *this* (pointing to the clean cotton puffing out of them) is our powder, and the cowries (the little shells which are the currency of the country), which are the proceeds of the operation, are the shots which England, the warmest friend of Africa, earnestly desires she should receive largely."

The spiritual work also made the labourer's heart thankful as he saw these natives professing faith in Christ, and in their lives and death exhibiting the power of the Gospel. One young female slave who had been ransomed by Crowther, and had embraced Christianity, died happily in the Lord, and others followed with a like encouraging testimony.

When the old king, Ama Abokko, died, the mission at Gbebe lost a good friend; and although his last words to his sons were to commend the work to their protection, his decease marked its termination. One of those fierce tribal wars which are constantly ravaging the country swept over Gbebe two years afterwards, and the town with its mission premises was utterly destroyed. The Christian converts were scattered, and a new station was as soon as possible started at Lokoja, on the other side of the river. Other troubles fell upon the work. Idda had to be given up through the treacherous conduct of a chief, who made a prisoner of Crowther and his son, the present Archdeacon, and demanded from the English a considerable sum for their ransom. They were, however, rescued, but unhappily not without the loss of a valuable life, that of Mr. Fell, the English Consul, who was shot by a poisoned arrow and killed.

In the meantime the work in Yoruba was making progress, and Crowther had translated into his native tongue not only the Bible, but other works, including the Prayer Book, and a Dictionary which will be of inestimable service to workers who shall follow in the field; others had translated the *Pilgrim's Progress* and the *Peep of Day*.

The ancient capital of the Yoruba district was Oyo; and here, in 1851, Mr. Townsend and his devoted wife, accompanied by Mr. Mann, another missionary, had an interview with Atiba, king of Yoruba, and in the illustration which we give of the scene it will be observed that a sacrifice of four human beings took place in honour of the visitors. These Egbas are Monotheists, although the Supreme Being is known amongst them by a variety of titles, as Olurun, the Prince of Heaven; Eleda, the Creator; Alagbura, the Powerful One; Oludomare, the Almighty; Oluwa, the Lord; and Elami, the Prince of Life. Their salutations are reverent; and on parting with anyone they say, "I remember you, and commit you to the care of God." It is common amongst them to use the native equivalent for "God bless you."

Mr. Townsend says that these people never worship the stars or heavenly bodies, and that one day, pointing to one of their idols, he asked the chief, "Why do you worship that image when you know it was cut out of a piece of wood by a man?" "I know it was carved by a man. I don't worship it." "But I have seen you worship it." "I don't worship the image, but the spirit that dwells in it." "What does that spirit do for you?" "He is my messenger to carry my petitions to God."

Sacrifices sometimes of human beings are made to

this idol, Shango. The illustration given on page 99, of the sacrifice of a sheep is singular, as after getting it to eat some plumtree leaves as a mark of acceptation, the animal is slain, and its blood scattered over the idol; also the brows of those performing this worship are marked therewith.

We must just add another instance to show the belief of these people in Divine Providence. There had been a fight between the warriors of Abeokuta and Ijaye and those of Ibadan, and the priest thus put it, the farmer, of course, referring to the defeated party :—

"A farmer went to clear a piece of ground on his farm for cultivation. Addressing a large tree that stood in his way, he said, 'To-morrow I will cut you down.' The tree, full of trouble, told God of it, saying, 'The farmer says he will cut me down to-morrow.' To which God replied, 'Be contented, he cannot.' The farmer returning home met with an accident, and was unable to resume his work for a long time. Then he repeated his threat, but with the same result; and now he was laid aside by a long illness. The third time he cleared his farm, and again addressed the tree, 'Tree, to-morrow, God willing, I will cut you down.' The tree, again addressing God, repeated the farmer's words, to which God answered, 'Did he say so? then he will do it.' On the morrow the tree was cut down." The point is that as long as the farmer trusted in his own strength he failed, but when he said, "I will, God willing," he succeeded.

We have now reached a point when we find Crowther once more in England. He had come to plead his own cause on the platform of our English May Meetings, and was the principal attraction at the Annual Meeting of the Church Missionary Society at Exeter Hall. The excited interest of that immense gathering was in a great part due to the fact that a negro, one of the very race from the distant African regions, was to tell his own tale. And a plain straightforward and effective speech it was. It was a remarkable evidence of the power of Christianity, a unique blending of the pleader and the example of the good of the cause at the same time. In the course of his remarks he said :—

"On one occasion I was travelling with the late lamented Bishop Weeks, then a simple minister. I went with him on a visit to a friend in the country. While I was in the railway carriage with him, a gentleman attacked him, knowing that he was a friend of missions. The gentleman said, 'What are the missionaries doing abroad? We don't know anything about their movements. We pay them well, but we don't hear anything about them. I suppose they are sitting down quietly and making themselves comfortable.' Mr. Weeks did not say anything in reply, I having made a sign to him not to do so. After the gentleman had exhausted what he had to say, I said to him, 'Well, sir, I beg to present myself to you as a result of the labours of the missionaries which you have just been depreciating;' and I pointed to Mr. Weeks as the means of my having become a Christian, and having been brought to this country as a Christian minister. The gentleman was so startled that he had nothing more to say in the way of objection, and the subsequent conversation between him and Mr. Weeks turned upon missionary topics. On the banks of the Niger, where we have not been privileged to be ushered in by European missionaries, native teachers have maintained their footing among their own people. Their countrymen look upon them as very much superior to themselves in knowledge and in every other respect, and listen to them with very great attention when they preach to them the Gospel of our salvation."

On St. Peter's Day, 1864, perhaps the most important event of his life took place, when in Canterbury Cathedral Samuel Crowther was consecrated as the first Bishop of the Niger. The scene was a memorable one, and is not likely to be forgotten by those who stood in the vast crowd which filled every aisle of the grand cathedral that day. The license of Her Majesty had been duly promulgated in these terms :—

"We do by this our license under our royal signet and sign manual authorise and empower you the said Reverend Samuel Adjai Crowther to be Bishop of the United Church of England and Ireland in the said countries in Western Africa beyond the limits of our dominions."

When the service began it was an impressive sight to see the Archbishop of Canterbury, attended by five other Bishops, enter the choir; and following them the three Bishops to receive the solemn rite of consecration, viz: the new Bishop of Peterborough, the new Bishop of Tasmania, and the new Bishop of the Niger. Remembering, as doubtless many did, the touching history of his childhood and early struggles as a slave, not a few in that vast building were moved to tears as

the African clergyman humbly knelt in God's glorious
house to receive the seals of the high office of Shepherd

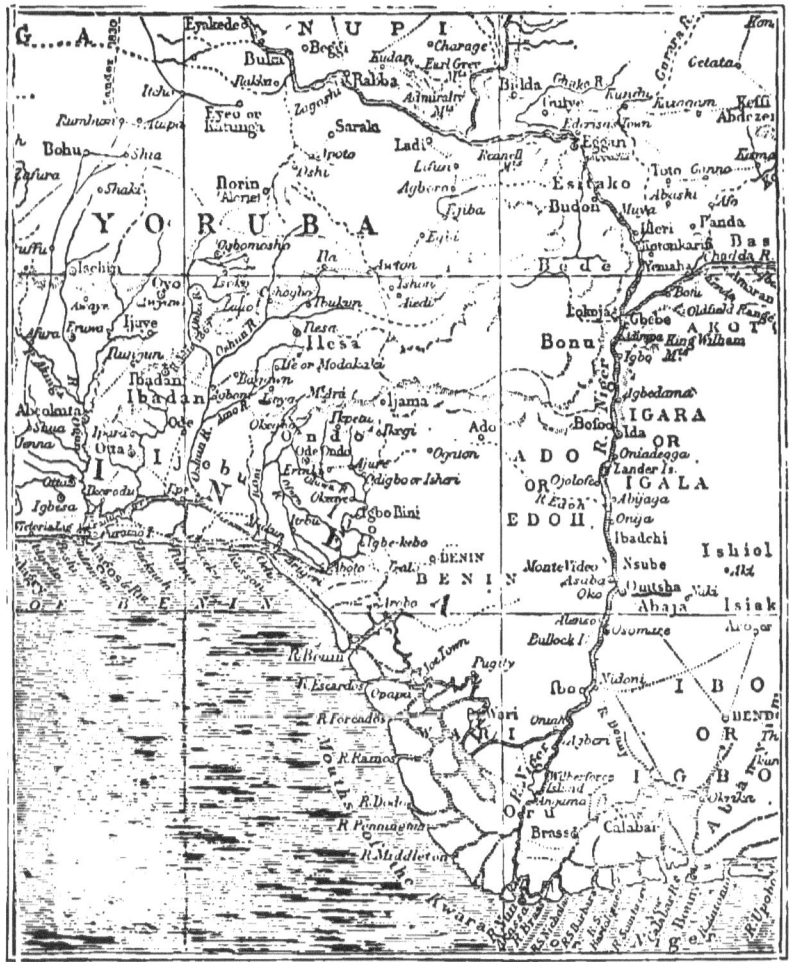

THE FIELD OF THE YORUBA AND NIGER MISSIONS.

in His earthly fold. Most of all must one heart have
been affected, that of Mrs. Weeks, the missionary's

wife, at whose knee he received his first lessons in the way of the Lord.

No one could fail to see how God had called forth this native from the degradation of a boyhood of slavery, to become a chosen vessel in His service. He had proved himself as a true-hearted standard-bearer of the Cross in much toil and patient endurance, and it was meet that to him should be committed the spiritual interests of the district in which he had spent hitherto nearly the whole of his life since he became a Christian.

On his immediate return to the Niger, the work began afresh with renewed energy. Special attention was given to the Delta, for King Pepple, having been on a visit to England, made an application to the Bishop of London to send missionaries to his dominions. A more degraded district was not to be found in Africa. Although its trade was very flourishing, being one of the chief markets for palm oil, the people were sunk in the lowest vices and superstitions. At the time of which we speak, when Bishop Crowther was forming the Christian Church there, the shocking practice of cannibalism was not yet wholly given up, and the people were entirely under the power of the priests of the Juju or fetish worship. As in Dahomey, no regard for human life seems to have existed; men were sacrificed at every high festival, and at the burial of any of their chief men a number of poor creatures would be slaughtered. The ghastly spectacle of their temple, paved and elaborately decorated with human bones, showed the ferocity of their religion.

In the midst of this awful darkness came Bishop

Crowther and his fellow-helpers, bearing the light of
the Gospel, and in due time many believed and were
saved. It was as in the early Church of the first
centuries, the adherents of the new religion were
mostly slaves, and to escape their persecutors had
to meet for worship and counsel in retired places.
The little Mission Church of St. Stephen's was
opened on the 1st January, 1872, and from time to
time converts were baptized, and the little assembly
of believers increased. But the superstition of the
priests and their votaries constantly made the little
church the object of their persecuting hatred. Again
and again its members were compelled to meet in the
secrecy of the forest for prayer. The hour of martyrdom had come ; some few could not stand the test,
but very many gloriously held faithful to their Lord.

One instance of this is the case of Isiah Bara and
Jonathan Apiafe, who were important persons in
their country before they embraced Christianity.
From that moment, however, they were bitterly persecuted, and finally, for the crime of carrying the
body of a poor Christian slave to burial, they were
publicly impeached by the Juju priests. Offered meat
sacrificed to idols, they preferred death to such dis-
honour of their Lord. Then they were bound with
chains, and put in a shed in the bush to die of star-
vation ; but in secret some of their brethren conveyed
to them a little food at the risk of their own lives.
When tempted, first by offers of honourable and
influential positions among the chiefs, and then by
threats of horrible punishment, their replies are
among the brave words of Christ's witnesses well
worth recording: "I have made up my mind," said

one of them, " God helping me, to be in chains, if it
so please the Lord, till the coming of the judgment
day ; " and said the other, fired with a like heroism,
" You know I never refused to perform my duty; but
as for turning back to heathen worship, that is out
of my power, for *Jesus has taken charge of my heart,
and padlocked it, and the key is with Him.*" For
twelve months these faithful ones endured this painful bondage, until relieved at last by the urgent
appeal of some English traders ; and they looked, on
emerging out of their captivity, more like wasted
skeletons than men.

Under such circumstances Bishop Crowther and
his son, Archdeacon Dandeson Crowther, appealed to
the Christians everywhere to aid the suffering mission
with their prayers, and from all parts of the world
letters of sympathy reached them, and in Tennyson's
figure we may say, the golden chains of prevalent
prayers bound once more the round world about the
feet of God. A special prayer-meeting was held, too,
at the Delta ; and, after it, the Archdeacon hastened
to the chiefs to ask them to withdraw the persecuting
hand against the Christians.

Three years afterwards the wife of a chief who
called himself Captain Hart, died. She had been the
very Jezebel of the persecution, and had urged her
husband to kill many Christians. Vainly did Crowther
seek access to her on her death-bed, the priests, to
whom she had always given largely of money and
presents, prevented this. When she had breathed
her last, the chief, her husband, was inconsolable,
and was grieved to think that his Juju idol had failed
to save her. Crowther found him, and tried to com-

fort the broken-hearted man. He says, " After
expressing our sympathy, I added that all the words
of comfort we can tell him will fail to heal the sore
in his heart; but we who are believers in Jesus
Christ have a 'balm' which heals such wounds; there
is a Physician, above every earthly physician, who
administers it into our hearts, and a change takes
place for good. Should he like us to tell him of that
balm for his broken heart?" He answered, " Yes,
tell me, and I will listen to you." After reading from
the book of Samuel, of the punishment of David's
sin, Mr. Crowther tells us he "turned to Psalm li.,
and carefully read the whole to him, and concluded
by pointing him to Jesus Christ, who has shed His
blood for us all, for him (the chief), for me, for every
man, and he that believeth in His name shall be
saved. I closed my Bible, he sighed and said, 'God's
word is true and is good. Come at another time, and
tell me more.'"

The death of his wife, the failure of his gods and
priests to deliver him in his trouble, and, most of all,
the good words of the Lord, had such an effect on the
chief that some time afterwards, when, in his turn,
he waited death, a striking scene took place. He
renounced his faith in his idols in the most distinct
manner, ordering them to be thrown into the river.
This was done on the day of his funeral, and the
people in a great fury wreaked their vengeance on the
luckless jujus, dashing them into the river and break-
ing them up into fragments. Thus this Ahab died,
and his household gods were scattered abroad.

The most popular of the gods of Yoruba is Ifa,
and a very interesting account is given by the Rev.

James Johnson, the native African missionary, of the conversion of one of its priests or medicine men. The man was growing into old age when he appeared before the Christian teacher as a seeker after truth. He had been for years in the habit of using his idol Ifa as a charm against the diseases of the people, but he himself had a painful malady which his idolatrous offices failed to cure. It so happened, however, that Jonah Shekere, who was a communicant of the Ake congregation, met him one day, and told the disconsolate Babalawo Dosimu that prayer to God through the Lord Jesus Christ would be more likely to cure him than all his charms and divinations. By appointment they met, and these two natives knelt together to ask the Great Physician if it was His will to take away the affliction from which Dosimu was suffering. God was not inattentive to their cry, and soon afterwards the sickness abated, and the poor repentant heathen found that rest and sleep, which for so long a time had forsaken him.

His Christian friend read to him the story of Jonah, and this greatly impressed him; and, although at such an advanced age, he begged to be instructed how to read, that he might know for himself more of the wonderful teaching of the Word of God. He renounced his idolatry, and brought to the missionary his Ifa or idol, saying, "I cannot tell how much I have spent in vain upon this useless thing! I sought recovery from it in illness, and it promised it; but its promises and assurances have not been fulfilled. Prayer to God has been of real help to me. I renounce Ifa, and will follow Christianity, that the Lord may give me perfect recovery."

As the light slowly dawned upon his benighted spirit, he spoke in a manner of his former worship, which is not unusual with these heathen priests after their conversion. "Such answers to prayers," said he, " I have found to be not answers from Ifa, who I had prayed to, but from God Himself, whom I ignorantly addressed as the holy, sinless, and good One, when I addressed Ifa thus, and was pleased to apply to Himself the prayers and addresses offered in simple faith though in ignorance to a thing that could not help."

Mr. Johnson, the missionary, thus concludes his sketch of this striking change of heart and life. "Dosimu attributes his conversion entirely to God. 'What else,' he says, 'could have brought me?' His chief anxiety is to be baptized, 'pinodu,' as he calls it. Pinodu is an abbreviation of, 'Pa-ina-Odu,' to kill, or put out the fire of Odu. Odu is a companion of Ifa, and is represented by charcoal, powdered camwood mixed with water and mud. He is the god who afflicts mankind with sickness and other troubles, and is said to be always in wrath against them. This wrath is 'ina' fire. To put out this fire is to propitiate him, remove his wrath, and secure his favour, and exemptions from his inflictions. Propitiation is made in a priest's house with the blood of a goat or sheep, and fowls slain at night at the time of offering. When Dosimu says he wants to 'pinodu,' he means to dedicate himself to God in baptism."

CHAPTER XI.

BONNY A BETHEL.

———✳———

"O come thou radiant Morning Star,
   Again on human darkness shine;
Arise, resplendent from afar,
   Assert Thy royalty divine:
Thy sway o'er all the earth maintain,
And now begin Thy glorious reign."—ANON.

———✳———

AFTER the passing away of Captain Hart and his persecuting wife, there came to the infant church at
Bonny another season of peace and prosperity. The
native schoolmaster sent to Bishop Crowther a joyful
report, thanking God that "Bonny has become a
Bethel." The destruction of Captain Hart's idols
made a salutary impression upon the minds of his
friends and neighbours. "His household — men,
women, and children—came with great joy to the
house of God."

While in times past the church had been harassed
by the animosity of such a Jezebel as the late chief's
wife had proved to be, it was now comforted by a
woman of considerable position and influence in the

place, who, receiving the Gospel in her heart, lost no
time in helping the good work with all her power.
In her house, every morning and evening, a large
concourse of people, chiefly of her own establishment,
met for family prayer. So greatly did the mission
extend that another church was built, and these were
both crowded, at every service, by people thirsting for
the Word of God.

This important station was placed under the care of
Bishop Crowther's son, the Archdeacon, and he
gathered the chiefs together and endeavoured to
persuade them to exercise at any rate toleration towards the mission. An event, however, of considerable importance occurred about this time.

The titular king of Bonny, George Pepple, had gone
to England for his health; and during his stay on our
shores had been everywhere received with respect and
enthusiasm. He made friends with the Lord Mayor
of London, was even introduced to the Prince of
Wales, and gave several addresses upon the subject of
his country's welfare, and the pleasure he felt at being
so well received. The most important feature of his
visit, however, was the interest evinced by all with
whom he came in contact in the mission work at
Bonny, and he was not slow to show his earnest
appreciation of its value and success. He must have
felt some twinges of conscience when he remembered
the persecutions the Christians had been subjected
to, and which no doubt he might have repressed
had he not stood in such fear of his chiefs. But now
that with renewed health and so many pleasant
recollections he was about to return to his native land,
he determined to take up a definite position as the

protector of, and sympathiser with, the work of Christianity in his kingdom. So this royal convert sent the following letter in advance to Archdeacon Crowther, announcing his return :

"Forgive me for not writing you prior to this. I will make it all right when I meet you in Bonny. People have made inquiries about you, and I have given them the best possible account. I shall be coming by next steamer, if it please God to allow me, and I wish you to get ready for a special service at the Mission church in Bonny. From the steamer (D.V.) I will proceed to the church to offer my thanksgiving to God."

In due time he arrived; and at the service which he attended, a special prayer of thanksgiving to God was read, and an earnest and impressive discourse preached by Archdeacon Crowther on the text from the Psalms : "Come and hear, all ye that fear God, and I will declare what He hath done for my soul."

The people, greatly encouraged by this action of their king, flocked to the mission, and worked with a will to erect fresh premises. In its after experiences, Bonny became one of the most encouraging stations in the district of the Lower Niger. On the pastoral visit of Bishop Crowther, a service was held in St. Stephen's Church, which, as described by his son in one of his reports to the parent Society, can only make the reader exclaim, "What hath God wrought?"

The *Formosa* had steamed from Brass, and had the Bishop on board. Then we are told, "Notice had already been given at the church the last Sunday of the expected arrival of the Bishop, who would preach, and a public examination of the children at school

was to take place afterwards. The following Sunday
(24th) came, the morning opened gloomily, but the
feathered songsters warbled out their praises to God
so cheerfully that morning, as if indicative of the
many voices which would be raised in jubilant praises
to God in His once neglected sanctuary.

"The tones of the church-going bell announced
the approach of the hour of service, and hardly had
the first bell stopped ringing when I saw on my way
to St. Clement's, by the beach path from Bonny,
scores of people hastening to St. Stephen's to secure
seats before the sound of the second bell. I returned
from St. Clement's, and found the Bishop preaching.

Turning to the congregation, a sight never witnessed before at Bonny met my eyes. The church was densely crowded—seats provided, and extra ones, closely packed to the pulpit and reading-desk, were filled. The pews filled, the gallery well occupied by the children, and the steps to the gallery lined with people. King George was present with his sister, Chief Fine Country, and other minor ones were there also, with the rich woman already spoken of, who, though ill during the week, yet was present at church. No less than 503 persons were attentively listening to the sermon, the Bishop telling them of the wonderful works of God among the people in the interior coun-tries of the River Niger.

"At the mention by the Bishop of such names as Mkpo, Umu-oji, Nknere nsube, Aron, Elugu, etc.—that the people of these places are sending messages to the mission at Onitsha, and that our agents are now travelling thither occasionally—one could notice the smiles and nods of approval from these poor listeners, many of whom had been caught and sold from the towns mentioned, and hence the joy to know that the Gospel will some day reach their own country.

"In the afternoon the Bishop again preached; and though the tide was high, above knee-deep over the beach path, yet there were 419 persons present."

One day two young converts appeared before Bishop Crowther at the mission-house for the purpose of purchasing some religious books in their language. In answer to the inquiry, "From where do you come?" they stated their place of abode was "the Land of Israel." In further explanation of this strange name, they told the Bishop, "You do not know what changes are taking place at Bonny; yonder village Ayambo, is named the Land of Israel, because no idol is to be found in it. Though you may walk through the village, you will not find a single idol in it as an object of worship. All have been cleared out, and some delivered to the Archdeacon. So it is free from idolatrous worship; and if anyone who professes the Christian religion is not comfortable at Bonny town, he is invited to this village, named the Land of Israel."

The influence of the Christian religion was everywhere making way, and the good tidings of salvation were being carried up the country. About thirty miles from Bonny is the town of Okrika, where there is an important market. Here people, who had been to Bonny, carried the news of what God was doing amongst the people there, and the chiefs and natives of Okrika, although they had never seen a Christian teacher, built for themselves a church, with a galvanized iron roof, which would hold at least three hundred worshippers, and got a schoolboy from Brass to come and read the Church Service to them. They sent a pressing invitation to Bishop Crowther to come and visit them. His son, the Archdeacon, however, came in his place, and was received with enthusiasm, and preached to them in the Ibo language. A few days after he was shown over the town, and having brought a brick-mould from Bonny he got some clay, and explained to them the process of making bricks.

The results of his discourse on the choice between Elijah's God and Baal was soon seen. "A chief named Somaire, who had been hesitating, and happily was at church, came after service and shook my hands, and said, ‘Uka ogula tá,’ ‘palaver set to-day.’ I asked him, How? He answered, ‘You will know to-morrow.’

“ On Monday morning he came in a canoe containing a large and small box full of idols and charms, four other chiefs who are church adherents were with me. We all stood by the wharf, and there he told me that he had decided to follow Christ, to throw away his jujus, and have nothing more to do with such folly. I answered, ‘Good, may God strengthen your heart.’ ” But in course of time, the opposition and intrigue of the chiefs, who disliked the support which King George Pepple afforded Christianity, caused serious trouble once more in Bonny.

In 1883 a letter of complaint against the Mission was signed by a majority of the chiefs, and shortly afterwards this was followed up by open revolt, and the king was dethroned and exiled. The churches were ordered to be shut up and burned down, and the severest punishment was meted out to all those who would no longer sacrifice to the jujus or idols.

Such a persecution soon displayed the martyr heroism of the Christians of Bonny. Six women who would not recant, were put into a canoe and left helpless in the middle of the river, and several others were banished or murdered. Archdeacon Crowther was warned off from Okrika under pretence of a coming war, and it seemed for the time as though Satan had the work at Bonny helpless in his hands. But with deepest darkness the star of dawn appeared, and suddenly, in answer to many prayers, relief came. Her Majesty’s Consul, E. H. Hewitt, Esq., arrived at Bonny in August, 1884, with a commercial treaty signed by the chiefs of the oil rivers in the Gulf of Biafra, and in this was a clause giving absolute freedom to missionaries to establish stations free from molestation. This was signed by the rebellious chiefs of Bonny; and afterwards, at the suggestion of the English representative, a council of chiefs was established, which led to the unanimous reinstatement of King George Pepple as their rightful ruler.

The most important clause in the constitutional memorandum, drawn up and signed by the chiefs on the accession of their king, was that he should be "exempted from taking part personally in any ceremony that may be contrary to his religion." Thus there was peace once more in Bonny, and the kingdom of Christ continues to extend its gracious power among the people.

The kingdom of Brass is one of the outlets of the Niger, and it was in 1867 that Bishop Crowther first met with its king, Ockiya, on the river Nun. He was at once favourably disposed to Christianity, and begged for ministers and teachers to be sent to Brass to give the same blessings to his people as he had heard had come to his neighbours at Bonny, further up the stream. Here, then, Bishop Crowther laboured hard, and as a result many were added to the Church ; and so prosperously did Christianity win its way among the people that the Juju priests, like those of Ephesus, soon began to realise that their gains were gone.

A visitation of small-pox in the district gave them the opportunity to blame the Christian teachers for it, and forthwith was initiated a cruel persecution, as bitter as that which we have seen was waged

at Bonny. Once more the spirit of faith and trust
in God was exhibited amid trials hard to be borne.
One of the converts was bound and dragged to
a place where a sacrifice was being offered to an
idol, and there his persecutors stood with a drawn
sword over him demanding his recantation; but he
did not give way. The king was powerless to curb
this bitter outburst of his priests and chiefs combined.
But after nine years of labour and more than one
outburst of fanatical opposition, the Church at Brass
was well established.

When in his latter days King Ockiya decided to
make a solemn and public profession of Christianity,
he paid a visit to Tuwon village to be baptized. This
rite was administered by Archdeacon Crowther on
the first Sunday in Advent, 1879, the king receiving
the name of Josiah Constantine. But for years, this
native potentate had shown himself very friendly to
the introduction and progress of Christianity in his
dominions. In spite of his juju men, he utterly gave
up his idols, and the principal of these are to be seen
in the Mission House, Salisbury Square. In our
illustration these are as photographed at Lagos on
their way to England. The two men, on either side
of Bishop Crowther, are Josiah Bara and Jonathan
Apiafe, of whose brave and patient loyalty to their
Master we have already had evidence in these pages.

King Ockiya was enabled by the grace of God to
give up polygamy, a great sacrifice for a royal
African to make; and his example as a Christian led
to the conversion of several of his heathen priests,
who are now baptised believers in the Saviour's
name.

KING OCKIYA'S IDOLS ON THEIR WAY TO ENGLAND.

Not only is there a great spiritual quickening among the people, but their material prosperity is evident. When Bishop Crowther visited one of the chiefs, Samuel Sambo, he found his house beautifully furnished, in the European style, with every luxury. There was one apartment, however, more neatly garnished, in which a table and a number of forms were seen. This was the praying-room, where, twice a day, the chief gathers his large household for family prayer. This, too, in a land where at the time of Bishop Crowther's first visit, cannibalism and superstitions of the vilest sort reigned supreme.

These poor heathen, so lately possessed with a devilish worship and cruel practices, are now sitting clothed and in their right mind, a spectacle of the power of the grace of God, which is not without its lesson even to the English people at home.

A striking instance of the reality of the change is given by Archdeacon Crowther. These are his words. "A sailing vessel called the *Guiding Star*, with cargo consigned to one of the firms trading on the Niger, arrived outside the Nun bar. No pilot was sent out to bring her in, so the captain sent his boat with five men in to get one. The boat capsized on the bar, one of the sailors was drowned, and the rest clung to the boat. Being ebb tide they were drifted away to sea, past Brass; and by the time the flood set in they were away down by an opening called the Nicholas. Cannibals live in this vicinity, hence any unfortunate being cast on Nicholas shore must be given up as lost. These four sailors were drifted ashore there, and picked up by the natives. Providentially for them one of the Brass church converts, called Carry, had some trade business with the Nicholas people; and his boys, who also attend church, were there at the time. They hastened and reported to their master about the sailors. At once Carry went, and after a good long talk, and showing them how God had turned the Brass people from such shameful practices through the Word of God, he succeeded in rescuing the sailors, and returned them to their ship at the River Nun. Carry's words when he handed the sailors to the captain of the ship (with whom I had conversation two days after) were these: 'Had I not known God and have become a Christian, these poor men would not have been alive to-day; we thank God!' This is a testimony from the mouth of a captain of the effect of Christianity and the power of the Gospel."

The improvement consequent on the establishment of the mission at Bonny is exhibited everywhere. Several years ago Bishop Crowther, in his report to the Society, enlarged upon the gracious fruits of the work of God among the people. There has been, from time immemorial, a custom of making sacrifices whenever an expedition of war canoes starts for the capture of slaves along the river. The blood of the animals thus sacrificed was sprinkled on the canoes in order to propitiate the god of war; but in this report we note that the Christian converts as one man, refused to carry out these observances. In one case a priest, who was not a Christian, objected to do what was required on the ground of the useless folly of the thing; but the head chief failing to compel him, told one of his slaves to take the whip and punish him. This, however, the slave declined to do, and again another refused. In a great passion the headman took the whip himself, and with all his might and main fell upon the delinquent. After this, under the impression that the castigation he had inflicted had brought the priest to a more willing state of mind, he again ordered him to sacrifice, but this order he again disobeyed.

A short time after this the priest was admitted as a candidate for Christian baptism. We read in the words of Bishop Crowther that—

"Bonny is now wearing quite a new aspect in a religious point of view; great changes are taking place for the better; and notwithstanding the persevering efforts of some priests, backed by the influence of some leading chiefs, heathenism is on the wane: many sheds, sacred to the gods, are out of repair, and the great temple studded with human skulls is going to ruin, with little hope of its being repaired. ' Surely the wrath of man shall praise Thee, and the remainder of wrath shalt Thou restrain.'

"Since the reaction took place at the death of Captain Hart—that great patron of idolatrous system and zealous supporter of this temple of human skulls —the people have learned more and more to think of the vanity of idol worship; especially when this great patron of heathenism could not conceal the fact which he had at last discovered at his dying hour, namely, that *all the gods are lies:* and withal, solemnly warned all his adherents against putting their trust in them any longer, as they were all lying vanities; and to exonerate himself as having been the great leader in their worship, he seriously commanded them to destroy all the images and figures of the gods which might be found in his quarter of the town

after his death, that they might not be a snare and
an excuse to them through his former example in
worshipping them ; which order was executed to the
very word. Thus God caused the wrath of this man,
the great persecutor, murderer, and banisher of the
Christians, to praise Him, while He restrained the
remainder of wrath by his removal, that His cause
may run and be glorified.

"After this, the threat from a persecuting influential chief, to confiscate the property of a convert,
a rich woman of Bonny town, could not induce her
to sell any article to this chief on the Lord's Day,
though he had fully determined to punish her for
thus refusing to grant his request, on the ground of
religious persuasion of its being a breach of God's
commandment. This persecution was designedly
planned to ensnare her ; but he was disappointed."

CHAPTER XII.

THE FRUITAGE OF THE SEED.

" As labourers in Thy vineyard
Still faithful may we be,
Content to bear the burden
Of weary days for Thee.
We ask no other wages,
When Thou shalt call us home,
But to have shared the travail,
Which makes Thy kingdom come."—MONSEL.

IT will be remembered that Bishop Crowther is a
Yoruba by birth and parentage, and, as might be
expected, there has ever been in his heart a special
yearning for the blessings of the Christian faith to be
vouchsafed to his own people and land. His visit to
Abeokuta, in 1846, has already been referred to in
these pages, when he was accompanied by that noble
co-worker, Mr. Henry Townsend.

This worthy missionary, who has not long gone to
his honoured rest, deserves something more than a
mere reference in this record of labour for Christ in
West Africa. He was a native of the cathedral city

of Devonshire, and his church in Abeokuta, being the
gift of his many earnest friends, was called the
Exeter Church. He was for six years a schoolmaster
among the freed slaves at Sierra Leone; and prompted
by a strong desire to explore the unknown regions of
the Yoruba country, from which many of the escaped
slaves, like the future Bishop of the Niger, had come,
he started for Abeokuta, the headquarters of the
nation. He was the first white man to enter its gates,
and his reception by Shodeki, the king, was remarkable for its cordiality. The people were as a field
white unto the harvest, so great was their desire for
light and truth.

One striking instance of this must suffice. Mr.
Townsend tells us in his journal: " Towards evening a
large party encamped as on the previous evening, and
after they had eaten and made themselves comfortable
I spoke to them. I said, ' Do you know the true God
who made us all, and preserves us day by day?'
'No; but we heard about ten years ago that white
men knew Him, and we have wished they would come
and teach us.' ' Do you want to know Him?' ' Yes.'
' Then you must ask God to send you teachers, and
He will send them to teach and lead you in the right
way of God.' They arose, and lifting up their hands,
said, ' O God! send us teachers to teach us about
Thee.' What more gratifying circumstance could
there have been than this. We were clearly called to
teach these people, and the result has further proved
it. Many who were then in heathen darkness have
since received the Gospel, and have died rejoicing in
Christ, trusting in Him alone for salvation."

After this visit, Townsend returned to England, and

after being fully ordained, was appointed to the mission at Abeokuta, and with Crowther re-entered the city in 1846. From that time it became the field of his special labours, although Crowther from time to time assisted in the establishment of the native church. The Egbas, who had securely entrenched themselves in this city, were continually being attacked by their old and remorseless foes, the Dahomians; and although in seven different campaigns the enemy ravaged the towns of the country around, still Abeokuta held out successfully.

In these onslaughts by the king of Dahomey, whose cruel and bloodthirsty character had began to shock Europe, the Christian converts whenever outside of the city, fell into his hands, and suffered many trials. One of them, named John Baptist Dasalu, was made prisoner at the repulse of the Dahomey attack in 1851, and was for twelve nights fastened to the ground with forked sticks, and then, after cruel torture, was sold as a slave, and sent to Cuba, where, on the application of the English Government, he was released. Another Christian Egba suffered martyrdom by crucifixion like his Lord; and not a few others had their portion of persecution and captivity.

In connection with the atrocities of Gezo, the king of Dahomey, a very pleasing incident is on record of the escape of a little girl from an awful death. It was in 1850, when Commander Forbes of H.M.S. *Bonetta*, was charged with a special mission to the king to induce him to put down slavery in his kingdom. In this excellent quest he was unfortunately unsuccessful, and during his short stay in the country, at the king's court, he saw with his own eyes what a number of lives were sacrificed to please the whim of this inhuman ruler. He was present at the custom known as Ek-que-noo-ah-toh-meh, at which sacrifice fourteen men in white dresses, with high red night caps, bound and placed in small canoes or baskets are flung by the king's own hand over a precipice, and then decapitated by his servants below.

Two years before this the king's army had utterly destroyed Okeodan, a city of the Yoruba country, in the same manner as Crowther's native town was destroyed in his childhood. Twenty thousand captives formed the spoil of the conqueror; and among them was a little girl whose parents had been killed, and she was only spared for a special sacrifice. This child was given by the king to Commander Forbes to take back as a present to Queen Victoria. She was baptised by the name of Sarah Forbes Bonetta, and educated at the Church Missionary Female Institution at Sierra Leone. After a few years, at the Queen's direction, she was brought to England to finish her education, and was in the care of Mr. and Mrs. Schön at Chatham. She soon became greatly loved, being of a lively, quick disposition, and was really promising in her English, French, and German studies.

It is quite characteristic of the Sovereign Lady who so happily rules this realm, that this little Yoruba girl was never lost sight of by her, and at her Midsummer and Christmas holidays she was always at the Palace for a few weeks, returning with some new present from the Queen. Amongst others she had a gold watch, a turquoise ring, and a beautiful gold bracelet with the words: "From Queen Victoria to Sarah Forbes Bonetta." She was specially invited when the Guards returned from the Crimea; and on the marriage of the Prince and Princess of Wales she had a ticket to the Royal Galleries, accompanied with suitable apparel.

She married at Brighton a leading Lagos merchant, and became Mrs. Davies, and her first child was named Victoria. On her return to her native country she became most useful in the mission work at Lagos, and died full of a joyful faith in her Redeemer, in September, 1880. The womanly sympathy of Her Majesty is so well known, that comment is unnecessary; but this brief but interesting incident must not close without an extract showing how the Queen received the news of the death of Mrs. Davies:—

"In August last (1880) Mr. and Mrs. Nicholson were staying at Sandown, in the Isle of Wight, and Mrs. Davies' daughter, Victoria (the Queen's godchild), who was in England for her education, was with them. While there the news arrived from Madeira that Mrs. Davies was seriously ill, and that she wished the Queen to be informed. This was done, and the following day Her Majesty sent for Victoria to come to Osborne. Just as she was starting thither with Mrs. Nicholson, the news came that her mother was dead."

Mrs. Nicholson writes: "I never shall forget the deep emotion shown by our beloved Queen when I gave her the letter announcing Mrs. Davies' death, and the motherly sympathy she expressed regarding her, saying with deep feeling, 'She was such a dear creature.'"

The constantly recurring wars have greatly hin-

dered the progress of the Mission; and during an
outburst in 1867, all the missionaries were expelled,
and the Mission premises destroyed. But in the providence of God the work was recommenced after the
lapse of a few years; and besides the church at
Abeokuta, a good work is being carried on at different
points in the country.

No event, perhaps, is so full of pathetic interest as
the passing away five years ago of the mother of
Bishop Crowther. We are told that this mother in
Israel never gave up entirely her native style of life,
she eschewed the European costume, and used to sit
by preference in the market-place at Lagos " like a
true Yoruba woman." To her, after a life of ninety-
seven years, the summons at last came; and " in
a happy condition, full of joy to go to her Saviour,"
this aged saint passed to that land where partings,
cryings, the weight of age, and the wrongs of slavery
never vex again.

In reviewing the work of the Mission on the Niger,
the practical mind of Bishop Crowther is stamped on
everything. In dealing with native races the spiritual
must be allied to the educational, and especially
where the wise course is being adopted of preparing
the converts themselves for work among their own
people. The foolish but prevalent idea, that the
African intelligence cannot develop under teaching,
is at once exploded by the spectacle of such a work
as is carried on at the Preparandi Institution at
Lokoja, situate at the confluence of the Binue and
Niger. This was started by the Bishop for the further
training of native boys as catechists and school-
masters. The stones to erect this substantial build-

ing were collected from the hills around, and the 15,000 pieces were carried by women to the mason who had been specially sent from Sierra Leone for the purpose of the work. Everything was paid for, and the sight of a number of men and women engaged in industry, properly remunerated, was a significant feature of that district. The place is a perfect marvel to the natives. They cannot understand how the stones keep together for such a height; and as they look in wonder, say to each other, "White man pass every man; white man, he next to God." It is quite on the College plan, with tutors' residences, dormitories, class rooms, and a printing room, the gift of the Society for Promoting Christian Knowledge. Such a centre of spiritual and educational activity will influence to an untold extent the future of the West Coast of Africa.

An apt illustration of how a little tact will overcome a difficulty is given in the case reported by the Rev. Daniel Olubi, of Ibadan in the Yoruba territory. At a small outlying station, Ogbomosho, there is a mission belonging to the American Baptists, and on the occasion of the burial of one of the converts a great riot ensued, the missionary who was making the coffin having to fortify himself in his house against the religious intolerance of the mob. The chapel, however, was speedily demolished, and even the pieces were taken away, so that in this emergency the missionary applied to the Church Missionary station at Ibadan, and Mr. Olubi sent a native Catechist, Mr. I. Okusende, to arrange the difficulty. After much opposition he managed to secure an interview with the Bale or headman, and learnt from him that a bitter feeling existed against the native Christians. They were accused of betraying the secrets of the Oro worship, and the Bale made many complaints which he had heard against them. This is what followed :

" Now why," said Mr. Okusende, " do you trouble yourselves about such things ? Why give heed to these foolish reports ? I beg," he continued, " that you the Bale and the Elders of Ogbomosko make two bags, long and large. One must be strongly sewn up, with a good thick bottom, but the other must be without a bottom. All reports and false accusations that would trouble you and agitate your town drop into the bag without the bottom, that they may fall through, but all beneficial and peaceful affairs put into the other." When he had finished, the Bale authorized his "Are Ago" (great chief) to welcome Mr. Okusende, and to wish him much blessing for the good message he had conveyed to them ; and then himself added, " We are not vexed with the teachers, but with our own people who go down to them to be taught and who reveal secrets of Epingun, Oro," etc., (these are well-known Yoruba superstitions.) " Stop," said Mr. Okusende, interrupting him, " such a word belongs to the bag with the hole, *drop it in.*" " Very well," the Bale replied, with a smile ; and after a few words he declared that all the suspicions and misunderstandings were now removed out of the way. " The town elders and myself," he said, " have done with them. The Church is again free and open as before, and all may attend who choose, and we will help in the rebuilding of the chapel."

We would commend the preparation of these receptacles to the attention of the white men and women at home, who, like the Bale of Ugbomosko, sometimes forget that of evil speaking a spark will kindle a whole fire of discontent and sorrow.

Reference has already been made to John Okenla, the brave chief of Abeokuta, who led forth his besieged fellow-countrymen, and inflicted a severe defeat upon the army of the king of Dahomey. He became the leading lay member of the Church at Abeokuta, and founded that interesting little Christian community lying between the city and Otta. For many years he held the post of Christian Balogun, and was always ready to take an active part in good works.

His end was sudden, but peaceful. He had borne well the weight of his eighty years, and on the Saturday before his death had walked twenty-five miles, and ten more on the Sunday morning early, so as to be in time for service at his church. He partook of the sacrament, and on the Monday following was present at the Harvest Thanksgiving service, bringing his own offering (twenty thousand cowries), and laying it in front of the communion rails. On the Thursday, after only two hours' illness, John Okenla fell asleep in Jesus, and at his grave gathered the native choir to sing a special song of mingled sorrow and joy, composed by one of their number. It was a touching scene, the strong men weeping bitterly at the loss of their old and faithful comrade. But absent in the body was present with the Lord, and John Okenla had gone to join that glorious throng who without ceasing praise the Lord.

A little lower down the river Niger than Onitsha, is the Ibo country, where a mission station has been successfully started by the converts of the former

place. On Easter Day, 1882, a very interesting visit
was made by about fifteen Christian Onitsha natives
to this place, when five hundred people gathered together to hear the strangers tell the wonderful story
of the Resurrection.

In the November following Bishop Crowther and
Archdeacon Henry Johnson visited Obotsi, and held a
service so impressive that the Archdeacon says, "My
heart did leap for joy on beholding the glorious scene
which unfolded itself before my eyes." An immense
semicircular concourse of chiefs and people were prepared to receive them. The greatest attention was
given to the sermon, the subject of which was the
Prodigal Son, and all joined in the sentences of the
Lord's Prayer, slowly read out to them in the Ibo
tongue.

One of the interpreters spoke to the people also
with eloquence and spirit, relating his experiences of
Christianity at Sierra Leone, and begging them to
find the Saviour. Quite 1,500 people were present,
and a number of Christian native women acted as
churchwardens in keeping order, and showing the
congregation when and how to kneel. The Bishop
was greatly encouraged with the result of his interview with some of his chiefs.

When the Bishop of Sierra Leone visited Port Lok-
koh, and other places of his diocese, in 1883, he had
an opportunity of talking with many of the chiefs
and headmen of the district. The remarks of one
of these were very significant, and showed a keen
appreciation of Christian privileges. Our laws he
admired because they made no difference between
rich and poor, and of the Bible he spoke with great

enthusiasm. His closing sentence will bear repetition, "The paper of your Book is light, but its words are heavy."

The eldest son of Bishop Crowther, the Archdeacon of the Lower Niger, paid a visit to England in the spring of the year 1883, in order to purchase two new churches for the Brass River, the amount required having been collected by the native Christians themselves. These churches were constructed of iron, carried in sections to Africa, and subsequently transferred in canoes to the places alloted to them up the river. When the church was commenced to be erected at Nembe, a vast concourse of people assembled to witness it rising piece by piece from the ground. The fixing of plates, equivalent to stone laying in England, was a scene to be remembered, and the special service which preceded it will not be soon forgotten by the assemblage of natives which gathered round. The chiefs and their wives, three hundred and fifty in number, formed a group round the spot where the banner of the Church Missionary Society waved in the wind. The native Clergy in their surplices, and the Catechist, occupied the small platform in the centre of the group; and after some devotional exercises, two leading chiefs, William Kennmer and Christopher Iwowari, members of the Church, spiked down the two corner plates, and the impressive formula, beginning "In true faith in the Lord Jesus Christ," was read by the Archdeacon. After a solemn prayer, committing the interest of the new sanctuary to the God of all grace and truth, whose house it was to be, all present rose and sang the Doxology.

It is a pleasing feature in the work of this Church, that a strong choir is gathered; and several beautiful hymns, such as Bickersteth's " Peace, perfect peace," and " Come to Jesus," are now translated into their own tongue.

In 1883, in the course of his pastoral visitation, Bishop Crowther accompanied Josiah Obuyanwuru, a Christian native, to Obitsi. They had with them nine female communicants, besides a number of young persons, and arrived at their destination in time to take the morning service in the new chapel built by the converts there, helped by generous and willing assistance from Onitsha. The building was of commodious size, thatched all along its sixty feet with bamboo matting. The service was begun by the singing of a hymn translated into their own language, read out to them verse by verse by George Anya-Ebunam, the interpreter. Then Josiah Obuyanwuru asked that some one would lead in prayer, and one of the female converts immediately offered an earnest supplication, praying for the conversion of the people, and specially mentioning the names of several of the leading men.

Afterwards Bishop Crowther preached on that watchword of missions, " Go ye, therefore, and teach all nations." The Bishop, in his own words, thus describes what follows: " After long speaking at the service, together with six miles' walk before on a gradual ascending land, I needed a little quiet rest for an hour or so, which I had, when a message came from Atta, one of the chiefs who was present at service, that he would be very glad to see me at his house, to which I consented to go. After the accustomed etiquette of offering the kola nuts and palm wine as marks of friendship and kind reception, the subject was broached, namely, their wish to be correctly informed whether what the Onitsha converts had told them in their preaching was correct, that, when any of their chiefs or persons of rank die, they should not keep the body for many days, during which time they keep up firing guns, drumming, and dancing until they obtain a slave for human sacrifice to be buried with the dead. The Christians never did such things, but quietly bury their dead as soon as possible. I confirmed the teaching of the converts as being quite correct, that at no death of a Christian in any part of the world would a human being be killed to be buried with the dead, how honourable soever the dead might have been in his lifetime, because this act is a great abomination in the sight of God ; neither would the relations of the dead make that an occasion of drumming, dancing, and firing guns for days, which I endeavoured to explain to them as utterly useless to the dead as marks of honour ; that if the dead be a Christian, as soon as his soul leaves the body he is carried by the angels into heaven, where he will enjoy everlasting happiness with Christ, who has washed the soul clean with His own most precious blood."

Death has been at work in different parts of the Niger district, gathering among the native converts many a shock of corn fully ripe. One of these was an old man, James Odernide, who was converted under the ministry of Mr. Hinderer at Ibadan. After thirty-five years of consistent witnessing for Christ, he was called hence after a long illness patiently borne. On one occasion, when the ministers were going to pray with him, he said, " You must not ask God to spare my life longer, for I should like much rather to be with Him before long." He longed for release, that he might enjoy the blessedness of being with Christ for evermore. Very full his heart was one morning when he exclaimed, amid his pain and weakness, " Would to God I were with Him to-day ! "

It is to be feared that too often the white man, when for the purposes of trade or exploration he enters the country of the heathen, does not show much evidence of the Christianity of the land from which he has come. He finds himself in the midst of a people who, degraded as they are, have a religion, and stand in awe of the god whom they ignorantly worship; but, although he has been brought up in the midst of surroundings of great enlightenment, there is no fear of God before his eyes. Thus it is that many natives learn, even before the missionary comes to them with the glad tidings of salvation, to despise the Christianity of the white man.

Again and again have Crowther's missionaries had to deplore the baneful results of the alcoholic drink exported from England to these heathen lands. Dense as is the darkness of superstition and cruelty among the poor people, we are, by our rum and gin, blotting out every lingering gleam of humanity and goodness from their lives and character. When the barrel has gone before the Bible, or after it, for the matter of that, the work of teaching the precious truths of the Christian faith becomes exceedingly difficult. That it is against the wish of the native rulers will be abundantly shown by the letter from a

Mohammedan king which we here transcribe. The original is in the Haussa language, written by Maliki, Emir of Nupé, on the Niger, two years ago, addressed to the Rev. C. Paul, a native missionary, to be handed to Bishop Crowther. The translation runs as follows:

" Salute Crowther, the great Christian minister. After salutation, please tell him he is a father to us in this land; anything he sees will injure us in all this land, he would not like it. This we know perfectly well.

" The matter about which I am speaking with my mouth, write it; it is as if it is done by my hand, it is not a long matter, it is about Barasa (rum or gin). Barasa, Barasa, Barasa! my God, it has ruined our country, it has ruined our people very much, it has made our people become mad. I have given a law that no one dares buy or sell it; and any one who is found selling it, his house is to be eaten up (plundered); any one found drunk will be killed. I have told all the Christian traders that I agree to anything for trade except Barasa. I have told Mr. McIntosh's people to-day, the Barasa remaining with them must be returned down the river. Tell Crowther, the great Christian minister, that he is our father. I beg you, Malam Kipo (Rev. C. Paul, native missionary), don't forget this writing, because we all beg that he (Bishop Crowther) should beg the great priests (Committee C.M.S.) that they should beg the English Queen to prevent bringing Barasa into this land.

" For God and the prophet's sake, and the prophet His messenger's sake, he (Crowther) must help us in this matter, that of Barasa. We all have confidence in him, he must not leave our country to

become spoiled by Barasa. Tell him may God bless
him in his work. This is the mouth-word from
Maliki, the Emir of Nupé."

In some cases, however, where the Gospel has been
already proclaimed in districts, Christian believers
are gathered together, and they gladly welcome any
who are in the fellowship of their common faith. A
very interesting incident of that is related of one of
the stations of the Niger. There, as we have seen,
native workers are in charge of the mission work, and
labour earnestly for the salvation of their brethren
according to the flesh. On one occasion one of the lay
agents of the Church Missionary Society, an European,
was visiting the great waterway of the Western Coast,
and being one evening at one of the stations, he took
part in the devotional services. He found, as is the
case everywhere, the natives were very fond of singing; and to their great delight he sang in solo some
of those hymns with which we are so familiar in
England, such as "Safe in the arms of Jesus," "Hold
the Fort," and others. The effect of this may be
understood by the words of the native missionary to
him afterwards. He said, "You greatly astonished
our people last evening. Though the station has been
in existence twenty years, you are the first white
man that they or I have heard pray or sing here.
We always tell the people that we are sent and supported by good white people in England to teach
them the Way of Life. But they, from having seen
the white traders so busily engaged about their trade,
and never attending or taking part in religious services, have drawn the conclusion that whilst teaching,
preaching, and worship are part of the white man's

religion, trading and getting money must be the
most important part of it, and to this, therefore,
he attends himself; but that preaching and teaching,
and generally the spreading of his religion, being
matters of minor importance, he pays black men to
attend to for him."

Surely such an impression, which is generally prevalent on the West Coast of Africa, should not be
allowed to continue to exist; and it is to be hoped
that the time will come when the increased interest
in mission work, and greater piety of our business
men both at home and abroad, will prove that we do
not in word only, but in very deed, "seek first the
kingdom of heaven."

In Lagos satisfactory progress is being made, and
the Native Pastorate Church, which is one of the many
blessed fruits of the work of the Church Missionary
Society, is distinctly gaining ground. In the Ebute
Ero Church, the members of which are all natives of
Lagos, a very interesting and encouraging event
occurred in September, 1878. The chiefs as they
joined the sanctuary, encouraged others to follow
them; especially was this the case with chief Ogubiyi, after whom came king Tiwo, of Isheri. This
royal personage was intimate with another chief,
Jacob Ogubiyi—who entered into fellowship with the
Saviour under the ministrations of a native missionary, the Rev. James White, and whose idols are
now at Salisbury Square.

When this Christian chief attended the early
morning service at the church, it was the custom of
king Tiwo to wait for him to come out, and it is
recorded that it was during his tarrying in the door-

way that some words from the native minister fell
upon his ear, which led to his conversion. He was
placed on trial for the baptismal rite, and in due
time the hour arrived when he should thus solemnly,
in the presence of his own people, enter Christ's
visible Church. The description of this scene was
given by a Lagos correspondent to the *African Times*
at that period, from which we quote the following
account :—

"Ebute Ero Church was not only crowded within,
but the church premises were densely thronged.
Among the crowd were several heathens and Mohammedans who came to witness the ceremony. After the
prayers the choir was singing a special hymn, when
the Rev. William Morgan entered the communion
rail, and king Tiwo came forward, suitably attired,
and stood in the front of the communion rail.

"After the Baptismal Service had been read, Tiwo
knelt down. It was a solemn, impressive scene, and
instructive to all, including our brethren, the heathens
and Mohammedans, when Mr. Morgan (one of the
sponsors), in the native tongue, said, 'Name this
person,' and Mr. Maser gave the name 'Daniel Conrad
Tiwo,' and he was baptized in the name of the Holy
Trinity. When the water was poured upon his head,
and the sign of the Cross made upon his forehead,
the heathen outside looking on, exclaimed in Yoruba,
'Olurun' (*i.e.* God), and the Mohammedans 'Allah'
(*i.e.* God), 'is great.' The sermon was preached by
Mr. Morgan.

"Tiwo soon gave evidence of his change of heart by
obeying the Divine command, 'Freely ye have received,
freely give.' He knew that as Christians we were
bound to do it by the examples of believers, both in

the Jewish and the Christian churches. Besides other
contributions, he freely gave £100 to the Ebute Ero
Church fund, and £25 to the building of the parson-
age house; and it was announced at the Bible meeting
on the 9th inst., that he gave two guineas as a thank-
offering.

" On hearing of his admission to the visible church
of Christ by baptism, his subjects and friends from
Isheri, Otta, and districts about Lagos, came to see
him, and he told them of the blessings of God; and
on Sunday, the 15th inst., no less than 560 persons,
male and female, including heathens and Mohammedans, went with him to church, 'and offered
thanksgivings for late mercies vouchsafed unto him.'"

To all who earnestly desire the extension of the
kingdom of Christ, this incident must convey a lively
sense of encouragement and gratitude. When it is
remembered that these are all black people, both
ministers and congregation, and that it was at this
very spot years before that Bishop Crowther was
carried a poor slave boy, the reader is constrained to
say, "What hath God wrought!"

The record of the closing years of his life is soon
told. During a brief stay in this country he wrote,
in his little room at Salisbury Square, that introduc-
tory letter with which these pages begin, invested
with a touching interest now that the hand which
penned it is still in death. After returning to his
diocese for about a year, he made one more visit to
England to consult a specialist about his eyes, and
this was the last time that his face was seen here.
Soon after his return to the Niger, troubles arose
there and the venerable Bishop strove with tact and
patience to restore unity between the native and